PENGUIN BOOKS

GREAT JONES STREET

Don DeLillo's novel *White Noise* won the National Book Award; *Libra* won the *Irish Times*–Aer Lingus International Fiction Prize; *Mao II* won the PEN/Faulkner Award. Don DeLillo is a member of the American Academy and Institute of Arts and Letters. The most recent of his novels is *Underworld*. Others include *Americana*, *End Zone*, and *Great Jones Street* (all available from Penguin).

Acclaim for *Great Jones Street*

"A major work of fiction . . . edifying, entertaining. . . . DeLillo does just about everything a novelist can do, with a sureness and an undiminished freshness."
— William Kowinsky, *The Boston Phoenix*

"A real novel of ideas, bursting with colorful inventions and enriched by a subtle groundwork of language and imagery which DeLillo brilliantly turns to the making of intricate abstract statements, and penetrating observations on the culture."
— *Library Journal*

"DeLillo is a powerfully disturbing writer . . . a full-grown talent, swift and tricky. . . . [Great Jones Street] is moving evidence of a writer stretching himself, accomplishing things he hasn't done before."
— Walter Clemons, *Newsweek*

"Chill atmosphere, satiric caricature and witty dialogue"
— *Time* magazine

"DeLillo spins his web, creates his own worlds, and has built the figure of his introspective, illogical, all-questioning anti-hero into a special kind of voice in a special kind of fiction."
— *The Irish Times*

Also by Don DeLillo

DON DeLILLO

GREAT JONES STREET

PENGUIN BOOKS

PENGUIN BOOKS

Published by the Penguin Group

Penguin Books USA Inc., 375 Hudson Street, New York,
New York 10014, U.S.A.
Penguin Books Ltd, 27 Wrights Lane, London W8 5TZ, England
Penguin Books Australia Ltd, Ringwood, Victoria, Australia
Penguin Books Canada Ltd, 10 Alcorn Avenue,
Toronto, Ontario, Canada M4V 3B2
Penguin Books (N.Z.) Ltd, 182–190 Wairau Road,
Auckland 10, New Zealand

Penguin Books Ltd, Registered Offices:
Harmondsworth, Middlesex, England

First published in the United States of America by
Houghton Mifflin Company 1973
Published in Penguin Books 1994

7 9 10 8 6

LIBRARY OF CONGRESS CATALOGING IN PUBLICATION DATA
DeLillo, Don.
Great Jones Street
Originally published: Boston:
Houghton Mifflin, 1973.
ISBN 0 14 01.7917 8
I. Title
PS3554.E4425G7 1983 813′.54 83–6928

Printed in the United States of America

GREAT JONES STREET

1

FAME REQUIRES every kind of excess. I mean true fame, a devouring neon, not the somber renown of waning statesmen or chinless kings. I mean long journeys across gray space. I mean danger, the edge of every void, the circumstance of one man imparting an erotic terror to the dreams of the republic. Understand the man who must inhabit these extreme regions, monstrous and vulval, damp with memories of violation. Even if half-mad he is absorbed into the public's total madness; even if fully rational, a bureaucrat in hell, a secret genius of survival, he is sure to be destroyed by the public's contempt for survivors. Fame, this special kind, feeds itself on outrage, on what the counselors of lesser men would consider bad publicity — hysteria in limousines, knife fights in the audience, bizarre litigation, treachery, pandemonium and drugs. Perhaps the only natural law attaching to true fame is that the famous man is compelled, eventually, to commit suicide.

(Is it clear I was a hero of rock 'n' roll?)

Toward the end of the final tour it became apparent that our audience wanted more than music, more even than its own reduplicated noise. It's possible the culture had reached its limit, a point of severe tension. There was less sense of simple visceral abandon at our concerts during these last weeks. Few cases of arson and vandalism. Fewer still of rape. No smoke bombs or threats of worse explosives. Our followers, in their isolation, were not concerned with precedent now. They were free of old saints and martyrs, but fearfully so, left with their own unlabeled flesh. Those without tickets didn't storm the barricades, and during a performance the boys and girls directly below us, scratching at the stage, were less murderous in their love of me, as if realizing finally that my death, to be authentic, must be self-willed — a successful piece of instruction only if it occurred by my own hand, preferably in a foreign city. I began to think their education would not be complete until they outdid me as teacher, until one day they merely pantomimed the kind of massive response the group was used to getting. As we performed they would jump, dance, collapse, clutch each other, wave their arms, all the while making absolutely no sound. We would stand in the incandescent pit of a huge stadium filled with wildly rippling bodies, all totally silent. Our recent music, deprived of people's screams, was next to meaningless, and there would have been no choice but to stop playing. A profound joke it would have been. A lesson in something or other.

In Houston I left the group, saying nothing, and boarded a plane for New York City, that contaminated shrine, place of my birth. I knew Azarian would assume leadership of the band, his body being prettiest. As to the rest, I left them to their respective uproars — news media, promotion people, agents, accountants, various members of the managerial peerage. The public would come closer to understanding my disappearance than anyone else. It was not quite as total as the act they needed and nobody could be sure whether I was gone for good. For my closest followers, all it foreshadowed was a period of waiting. Either I'd return with a new language for them to speak or they'd seek a divine silence attendant to my own.

I took a taxi past the cemeteries toward Manhattan, tides of ash-light breaking across the spires. New York seemed older than the cities of Europe, a sadistic gift of the sixteenth century, ever on the verge of plague. The cab driver was young, however, a freckled kid with a moderate orange Afro. I told him to take the tunnel.

"Is there a tunnel?" he said.

The night before, at the Astrodome, the group had appeared without me. Azarian's stature was vast but nothing on that first night could have broken the crowd's bleak mood. They turned against the structure itself, smashing whatever was smashable, trying to rip up the artificial turf, attacking the very plumbing. The gates were opened and the police entered, blank-looking, hiding the feast in their minds behind metered eyes. They made their patented charges, cracking arms and legs in an effort to protect the concept of regulated temperature. In one of the worst public statements of the year, by anyone, my manager Globke referred to the police operation as an example of mini-genocide.

"The tunnel goes under the river. It's a nice tunnel with white tile walls and men in glass cages counting the cars going by. One two three four. One two three."

I was interested in endings, in how to survive a dead

idea. What came next for the wounded of Houston might very well depend on what I was able to learn beyond certain personal limits, in endland, far from the tropics of fame.

4

2

I WENT to the room in Great Jones Street, a small crooked room, cold as a penny, looking out on warehouses, trucks and rubble. There was snow on the window ledge. Some rags and an unloved ruffled shirt of mine had been stuffed into places where the window frame was warped and cold air entered. The refrigerator was unplugged, full of record albums, tapes and old magazines. I went to the sink and turned both taps all the way, drawing an intermittent trickle. Least is best. I tried the radio, picking up AM only at the top of the dial, FM not at all. Later I shaved, cutting myself badly. It was strange watching the long fold of blood appear at my throat, collecting along the length of the gash, then starting to flow in an uneven pattern. Not a bad color. Room could do with a coat. I stuck toilet paper against the cut and tried with no luck to sleep a while. Then I put Opel's coat over my shoulders and went out for food.

It was dark in the street, snowing again, and a man in a long coat stood in the alley between Lafayette and

Broadway. I walked around a stack of shipping containers. The industrial loft buildings along Great Jones seemed misproportioned, broad structures half as tall as they should have been, as if deprived of light by the great skyscraper ranges to the north and south. I found a grocery store about three blocks away. One of the customers nudged the woman next to him and nodded in my direction. A familiar dumb hush fell over the store. I picked up the owner's small brown cat and let it curl against my chest. The man who'd spotted me drew gradually closer, pretending to read labels along the way, finally sidling in next to me at the counter, the living effigy of a cost accountant or tax lawyer, radiating his special grotesquerie, that of sane men leading normal lives.

I got back to find Globke with his arm down the toilet bowl.

"I dropped a dime," he said.

"The floor's not very clean. You'll ruin your new pants. What is that — vinyl?"

"Polyvinyl."

"And the shirt," I said. "What about the shirt?"

He struggled up from the floor, then held his stomach in and adjusted his clothes. He followed me into the main room, not exactly a living room since it included a bathtub and refrigerator. Globke himself occupied a duplex apartment in a condominium building situated on the heights just across the Hudson River. His apartment was a model abode of contour furniture and supergraphics, an apparent challenge to the cultured indolence of Riverside Drive. His second wife was young and vaporous, a student of Eastern religions, and his daughter by his first marriage played the cello.

"There's a story behind this shirt," he said. "This shirt is part of an embroidered altar cloth. Fully consecrated. Made by blind nuns in the foothills of the Himalayas."

"What's that color? I've never seen a shirt exactly that color."

"Llama vomit," he said. "That's what they told me when I bought it. There's a rumor you're dead, Bucky."

"Do you believe it?"

"I came here for the express purpose of letting you know, all kidding aside, that no matter what your intentions are, we're determined to see you through this thing, irregardless of revenues, monies, so forth — grosses and the like. Your own intentions are uppermost."

"I have no intentions."

"Contractual matters. Studio dates. Record commitments. Road arrangements. We go when you say go. Until then we sit with our legs crossed. What the hell, an artist's an artist. Bookings. Interviews. Press parties. Release dates."

"How did you get in here?"

"It wasn't hard to figure out you'd be here. I knew you'd be here. Once we traced you to New York, I knew this was where you'd be. But look how hollow-cheeked. Look how ghostly. I had no idea. Who knew? Nobody told me."

"But how did you get in here?" I said.

"I picked up the key on my way in from the airport. I've been in Chicago the past two days. First they tell me you've disappeared, so I make all the usual inquiries. Then they tell me there's a riot in the Astrodome, so I make all the usual public statements. Then I catch a plane to New York and pick up the key on my way down here."

"Pick up the key where?"

"At our lavish offices in world-famous Rockefeller Center."

"What was it doing there?"

"Transparanoia owns this building," he said.

"I didn't know we were in real estate. Since when?"

"Two or three months ago. Modestly. We're in very modestly. Lepp's a cautious man. He picks up a piece of property here and there. Mostly related to the business. An old ballroom or theater. Shuttered property. Nothing big."

"What are we doing with a building like this?"

"Lepp stays out of my sphere of influence and I don't go messing in his. I'm not in love with what you look like, Bucky. You're a morbid sight. A one-man horror movie. Where's Opel?"

"Don't know."

"I thought she'd be here. I don't see her all this time I figure she's in her funny apartment shooting God-forbid some kind of terrible drug between her toes, the only skin left."

"I haven't seen her in a while. She may be in Morocco, she may not. Then again she may."

"You plan to go looking?"

"I'm staying right here," I said.

"That's your right and your privilege, Bucky, with or without a studio-equipped house in the mountains. The first death rumor was in the evening paper. I could easily stop it here and now."

"I don't think you could. But either way, don't get into it. I want to see how long it lasts."

"Whatever you say."

8

"I haven't asked about your wife. How's your wife, what's-her-name, your lovely and charming wife?"

"Wife, companion, lover," Globke said. "She's all that and more. Mother, daughter, teacher, adviser, friend. But I'm keeping you two apart. Otherwise it's instant sex karma. She's got a beautiful soul but I don't trust her body. See, oldness and fatness. They make me a bad person."

"What's she do all day, stranded on top of that cliff?"

"She curls up with the *Upanishads*. She's been reading the *Upanishads* in paperback for the last three years. She feels the East is where the truth is, what she calls the petal of all energy. Non-attachment turns her on."

"And the little girl," I said.

"Still at it with the cello. Appreciate your asking. To think my genes could produce this kind of classical talent. She'll be concertized next year. Age of fourteen."

"Will it hurt?"

"You attack even the things I hold dearest, Bucky, but I forgive you because I know you're on the threshold of something extra-extra-ordinary or you wouldn't be here in this cold dark room far from the hue and cry. Or am I wrong?"

"Dead wrong."

"At least you could give me the mountain tapes. If you handed over the mountain tapes, I'd at least have something to play with."

"How's my band?" I said.

"The boys are confused. What can I say? The boys are confused, hurt and bereaved."

"Azarian's not bereaved. He's doing his little hip-flips right out front."

"With him everything's on the surface. He doesn't give it that extra level. I think they'll break up."

"Not for a while."

"Who needs them?" he said.

"They're valuable as artifacts."

"Bucky Wunderlick. That's what people want. In the flesh."

"I have to get some rest now."

"You're kicking me out. Listen, why not? It's been an emotion-packed twenty-four hours and you desperately need sleep. It stands to reason."

"Tell Lepp to get rid of this building."

"It's a business thing," he said. "Diversification, expansion, maximizing the growth potential. Someday you'll understand these things. You'll open your mind to these things. Someday you'll be thirty years of age and you'll have to go out and make an honest living, ho, like the rest of us."

"Never," I said.

"Ho, the ageless wonder. But what I wish you'd do is, talking of time and tide, is I wish you'd go back to writing lyrics, real lyrics the way you used to write them and sing them. That would amaze and delight the whole world, Bucky. A surprise return to your old self. There was nobody better at it."

"When are you leaving, Glob?"

"He throws me out right to my face. A spontaneous put-down. He is famous for this kind of thing but I stand here and take it because it has been an emotion-packed twenty-four hours and he is a star of the firmament while I am only his personal manager who took him out of the rain when he was a scrawny kid and made him what he is today, an even scrawnier kid. But just so you don't think I'm not appreciative of what you've been doing in the later stages, normal lyrics or no normal lyrics, I want you to know a few weeks ago wherever I was in the vast Southland I picked up HBQ Memphis on the car radio and they were doing 'Pee-Pee-Maw-Maw,' both sides, no commercial interruptions. Not that it's so unusual. I just want you to know I'm not all cash-and-carry. I relate to your sound. It's not my sound. It's not the sound I want my kid to make. But it's a valid sound and I relate to it."

"Love to all," I said.

I watched him make his way down the narrow staircase, prodigious in his width, haunches rocking in that firm eternal way of beasts of burden. I imagined him a few minutes hence, standing on the Bowery trying to hail a cab to take him to his car, a custom-made machine gleaming at the top of a circular ramp in some midtown garage. Globke was accustomed to being propelled, ballistically, to and from distant points of commerce, and so there was something agreeably serene, even biblical, in his rudimentary journey down those stairs.

I set the radio dial between local stations and picked up some dust from a delta-blues guitar far off in the night. After a while I had some soup and went to bed, wearing Opel's coat. I knew it was warm wherever she was, most likely a crowded city in one of the timeless lands she loved so much. She favored warm climates and teeming streets. In my mind she was always emerging from hotels in timeless lands and looking around for signs of a teeming street. She liked to watch Arabs spit, and was entertained by similar shows of local prowess in non-Islamic countries. Opel's father was a titled American — president of a small

Texas bank, board member of a utilities company, partner in an auto dealership. She fled all this for a life in rock 'n' roll. She wanted to be lead singer in a coke-snorting hard-rock band but was prepared to be content beating a tambourine at studio parties. Her mind was exceptional, a fact she preferred to ignore. All she desired was the brute electricity of that sound. To make the men who made it. To keep moving. To forget everything. To *be* the sound. That was the only tide she heeded. She wanted to exist as music does, nowhere, beyond the maps of language. Opel knew almost every important figure in the business, in the culture, in the various subcultures. But she had no talent as a performer, not the slightest, and so drifted along the jet trajectories from band to band, keeping near the fevers of her love, that obliterating sound, until we met eventually in Mexico, in somebody's sister's bed, where the tiny surprise of her name, dropping like a pebble on chrome, brought our incoherent night to proper conclusion, the first of all the rest, transactions in reciprocal tourism.

She was beautiful in a neutral way, emitting no light, defining herself in terms of attrition, a skinny thing, near blond, far beyond recall from the hard-edged rhythms of her life, Southwestern woman, hard to remember and forget. She went on tour with the band and we lived together in houses, motels and apartments, Bucky and Opel, rarely minus an entourage, the beds piled high with androgynous debris. There was never a moment between us that did not measure the extent of our true connection. To go harder, take more, die first. But before it could happen, Opel began her travels to timeless lands.

3

I DON'T KNOW exactly when it was that I became aware of footsteps in the room above mine. They were measured steps, falling lightly but in obvious patterns, suggesting a predatory meditation, as of pygmies rehearsing a ritual kill.

The mornings were cold and dark. Down the street the rounded doors of the firehouse remained closed except for one day at dawn when a truck nosed slowly out, its lights dissolved in low fog, silent men clutched to its sides, apparitional in black slickers. Derelicts were everywhere, often too wasted to beg. Many of them had an arm or leg in a cast, and the ones with bottles mustered sullenly in doorways, never breaking their empties, leaving them behind as they themselves moved north to forage, or simply disappeared. Two feeble men wrestled quietly, humming wordless curses at each other, and an old woman limped into view, bundled in pounds of rags, an image in the penciled light of long retreat from Moscow. I opened the window and touched the brittle crust of snow settled on the ledge. The fire engine went speeding down Broadway, pure sound now, shrill wind, a voice from the evilest dreams.

A boy named Hanes, the fairest of Globke's assistants, came to see me one afternoon. He brought mail, newspapers, contracts and some cash.

"You were seen in a drive-in restaurant in Ocala, Florida," he said.

Hanes was barely twenty, poetically delicate in appearance, and it was hard to imagine him at work in the Transparanoia offices, a place where squat men, outsweating the effects of air conditioning, were willing to hack off slabs of their own body fat to sell by the pound over transatlantic phone hookups.

"You were also seen at the airport in Benton Harbor, Michigan. According to the thing in the paper, the person who saw you walked up to you and said: 'Hey, Bucky, where you going?' And you said back: 'To get some Chinese food.' Then a two-engine plane rolled up and you got aboard."

Hanes sat on the edge of the unmade bed. His eyes never left me. I remembered a night on the West Coast some months before. The country's blood was up, this or that atrocity, home or abroad, and even before we hit the stage the whole place was shaking. We were the one group that people depended on to validate their emotions and this was to be a night of above-average fury. In our own special context we challenged the authenticity of the crowd's passion and wrath, dipping our bodies in coquettish blue light, merely teasing our instruments for the first hour or so. Then we caved their heads with about twenty thousand watts of frozen sound. The pressure of their response was immense, blasting in with the force of a

14

natural disaster, and it became even greater, more physically menacing, as they pressed in around the stage, massing for the holocaust, until finally it broke, all hell, and the only lucid memory I later had was of someone slightly familiar pushing across the stage, his face brilliant with pain, eyes clearly seeking me through every layer of chaos, Hanes, stopping now to punch the drums, whirling in his torn shirt, a sleeve hanging empty, Hanes himself, tumbling backward over a bank of amps.

"I've got a new Garrard changer," he said.

"Glad to hear it."

"My tone arm setup has zero tracking error."

"Do one thing for me," I said. "Take these contracts back."

That night there was a fire in an oil drum on the street below the window. Four people stood around the drum, occasionally tossing wood and garbage into the flames. I tried to read one of the newspapers Hanes had left. The words made no sense to me. I looked at the cover of a magazine and could not quite put together the letters in big block print. In time I fell asleep in a chair, remaining there after waking. There was a knock at the door. I went to the window and looked down to the street, where three of the people were still gathered, bouncing on their toes in the cold. The fourth was at the door, an ageless girl in defeated wet fur, trying to blink her way back to the realm of events. Her long druid's face rested on a package she carried high on her chest.

"I'm Skippy, Bucky. I just want to give you something from somebody and I won't hang around and bother you, I really promise and all. Can I come inside for a minute and no more?"

"But not your friends," I said.

"There's a body in the hall downstairs."

"Probably mine."

"First off this boy I know from New Mexico, Bobby from New Mexico, made me promise to tell you he knows where to get some unbelievable hash that you can have for nothing and you don't even have to talk to him. I'm pretty sure that's it — hash, for nothing, unbelievable."

"I turn on and off with the radio now."

"It's okay really because that's not the something I'm supposed to give you anyway."

She handed me the package.

"What is it?" I said.

"They want you to hold it here because they trust you and there's no other safe place. Someone will come and pick it up at the right time."

"Who wants me to hold it?"

"Happy Valley Farm Commune."

"What's that?"

"It's a new earth-family on the Lower East Side that has the whole top floor of one tenement. Some of them are ex-Desert Surfers."

"They don't trust each other. But they trust me."

"I guess so," she said. "Three of them are outside now. But they didn't want to come up. They want to show you they respect privacy. They want to return the idea of privacy to American life. They have shotguns, they have handguns, they have knives, they have blowtorches, they have army explosives, they have deer rifles. They stole whatever's in that package. I'm supposed to tell you that Dr. Pepper is going to analyze the contents as soon as they can find out where he is. So once they find him and either get him to Essex Street or go to wherever he is, someone

16

will come over here and get the package. I'm supposed to say Dr. Pepper, analyze, Essex Street, get the package. I'm pretty sure that's it."

"Your friends aren't too well organized, are they?"

"They're getting it together. It takes time, I guess. They're new to the city and all. But they think what you're doing right now is really something."

"What am I doing?"

"Returning the idea of privacy to American life."

"Nice seeing you," I said. "Always nice to see nice people. If you ever want the package and I'm either unconscious, dead or not here, have your friends kick in the door. I'll leave the package in an obvious place."

"My name's Skippy."

"I know."

"I can come back later if you want. Whatever you want, Bucky. I can bring my friend Maeve. Or I can come all by myself. Or I can just send Maeve."

"None of those," I said.

"Okay, real glad I came up and all. I was in Atlantic City when you did the four straight hours. Bobby from New Mexico was in Houston the night you weren't there. Said it was killer. Broke his left wrist jumping off a wall. Real ga-ga night. Okay, have to go now. Too bad we didn't get too much chance to really talk. But it's okay, Bucky. I'm nonverbal just like you."

From the window I watched her talk with the three men before all walked off in a light snow. I heard the footsteps again, someone pacing in a complicated pattern. The package was about twelve inches square, not heavy, wrapped in brown paper sealed with plain brown tape. I dropped it in a small trunk in a corner of the room. It took a long time for the fire in the oil drum to go out. I put on Opel's coat and waited for first light.

Slowly along Great Jones, signs of commerce became apparent, of shipping and receiving, export packaging, custom tanning. This was an old street. Its materials were in fact its essence and this explains the ugliness of every inch. But it wasn't a final squalor. Some streets in their decline possess a kind of redemptive tenor, the suggestion of new forms about to evolve, and Great Jones was one of these, hovering on the edge of self-revelation. Paper, yarn, leathers, tools, buckles, wire-frame-and-novelty. Somebody unlocked the door of the sandblasting company. Old trucks came rumbling off the cobblestones on Lafayette Street. Each truck in turn mounted the curb, where several would remain throughout the day, listing slightly, circled by heavy-bellied men carrying clipboards, invoices, bills of lading, forever hoisting their trousers over their hips. A black woman emerged from the smear of an abandoned car, talking a scattered song. Wind was biting up from the harbor.

I had the door half-open, on my way out for food, when someone spoke my name from the top of the next landing. It was a man about fifty years old, wearing a hooded sweat shirt. He was sitting on the top step, looking down at me.

"I've been waiting for you," he said. "I'm your upstairs neighbor. Eddie Fenig. Ed Fenig. Maybe you've heard of me. I'm a writer, which gives us something a little bit in common, at least retroactively. I write under my full name. Edward B. Fenig. You're tops in your trade, Bucky, looking at your old lyrics, never having attended a live performance. So when I saw you from my window yesterday when you were crossing the street this way, I was naturally delighted. Sheer delight, no exaggeration. Maybe you've heard of me. I'm a poet. I'm a novelist. I'm a mystery writer. I write science fiction. I write pornography. I write daytime dramatic serials. I write one-act plays. I've been published and/or produced in all these forms. But nobody knows me from shit."

Americans pursue loneliness in various ways. For me, Great Jones Street was a time of prayerful fatigue. I became a half-saint, practiced in visions, informed by a sense of bodily economy, but deficient in true pain. I was preoccupied with conserving myself for some unknown ordeal to come and did not make work by engaging in dialogues, or taking more than the minimum number of steps to get from place to place, or urinating unnecessarily.

4

AGAIN I had a visitor, four days into unbroken solitude, a reporter this time, flamboyantly bald and somewhat dwarfish, dressed in sagging khaki, drifts of hair from outlying parts of his head adorning the frames of his silver-tinted glasses, an emblem on the sleeve of his battle jacket — RUNNING DOG NEWS SERVICE.

"Where do you want to sit?"

"Your manager told us you were approachable," he said. "We've known for seventy-two hours where you were located but we didn't want to make a move until we got ahold of Globke. We don't operate mass-media-crash-style. We wanted Globke's version of your frame of mind in terms of were you or were you not approachable. I'll take this chair and we can put the tape recorder right here."

"No tape," I said.

"That's what we anticipated."

"No notes either."

"No notes?"

"Note-taking's out."

"You want some kind of accuracy, don't you?"

"No," I said.

"Then what do you want?"

"Make it all up. Go home and write whatever you want and then send it out on the wires. Make it up. Whatever you write will be true."

"We know it's asking a lot to expect an interview, even a brief one, which is what we assure you is what we want, but maybe a statement will have to do. Will you give us a statement?"

"A statement about what?"

"Anything at all," he said. "Just absolutely anything. For instance the rumors. What about the rumors?"

"They're all true."

"Okay, but what about authorities in Belgium?"

"Does Globke have Belgium under contract? If Globke doesn't have it under contract, whatever it is, I'd be guilty of malfeasance in discussing it publicly."

"Authorities in Belgium want to question you about your alleged financial involvement in a planeload of arms confiscated in Brussels that was supposedly on its way to either this or that trouble-spot, depending on which rumor you believe."

"Do you know what the word malfeasance means? This is a word that carries tremendous weight in a court of law. Much more weight than misfeasance or nonfeasance."

"Okay, but what about the damage to your vocal chords from the continuous strain and the story that you'll never perform in public again?"

"You decide, "I said. "Whatever you write will be true. I'll confirm every word."

"Okay, but what about Azarian? Azarian says he's reorganizing the group along less radical musical lines. Will you make a statement about that?"

"Yes," I said.

"What's your statement?"

"Azarian has been horribly disfigured in a gruesome accident. His face is being reconstructed with skin and bone taken from the faces of volunteers. His voice is not his voice. It belongs to a donor. What Azarian seems to be saying is really being said by another person's vocal chords."

"That's the other thing. An accident. You were in an accident and you're hidden away in some rich private clinic in south central Maryland. The accident thing was interesting to us, ideologically. An accident for somebody like you is the equivalent of prison for a revolutionary. We were kind of rooting for an accident. Which is, wow, really weird. But that's what happens. You get into guerrilla ideology, you find yourself trying to handle some pretty unwholesome thoughts."

"There's no such region as south central Maryland."

"Okay, but listen to this on the subject of accidents. We got a tip from I won't say what source that your manager was about to leak word of an accident. We figure he wanted to co-opt all the other accidents. He wanted exclusive rights to your accident. Anyway his story had you half-dead when a schooner piled into some rocks during a storm off the coast of Peru. First you're missing and presumed drowned. Then you're half-dead aboard a rescue vessel. And Peru does have a coast because I was there two years ago Christmas. But he dropped the idea for whatever reason. This is pretty sophisticated stuff, Bucky. I mean there's rumor, there's counter-rumor, there's manipulation, and there's, you know, this ultra-morbid promotional activity. What's it all mean?"

"The plain man of business is gone from the earth."

"Before I forget," he said, "we'd like to add your name to a list of sponsors that we use on all correspondence pertaining to the black captive insurrection fund. The other names are on this sheet. Should I leave it and you can get back to us or do you want to look at it now? It's up to you ,whatever you want me to do with it."

"Tear it in four equal pieces," I said.

"Okay, can we get on to some more statements now?"

"I don't think so, no."

"We'd like a short statement about your present whereabouts."

"I'm wherever you want me to be."

"We know where you are at this point. We want to know what you're doing here."

"Nothing."

"But why here?" he said. "Will you make a statement about that?"

"You know where you are in New York. You're in New York. It's New York. This fact is inescapable. In other places I didn't always know where I was. What is this, Ohio or Japan? I wanted to be in one place. An identifiable place."

"Okay, but you've got a studio-equipped house in the mountains and it's almost inaccessible to anybody who doesn't have a detailed map. We still don't see why you're here rather than there. You've lived there. It must be identifiable."

"How tall are you?" I said.

"Six feet even."

"Incredible."

"It's the way I hunch."

"You're a six-foot dwarf."

"I hunch. I can't help it. I've always hunched."

"It's really a studio-equipped mountain," I said. "There is no house as such. There's the facsimile of a house. There's the pictorial mode of a house. Exactly what my house in the mountains would look like if I had a house and there were mountains. My present state of mind doesn't accommodate the existence of mountains. I am in a plains mood."

"Can we discuss your personal life?" he said.

"Sure we can. I won't be here while we're discussing it because I'm going out now. But you go right ahead. Everything you report will be true. I'll personally vouch for every syllable."

"Your manager told us you were approachable."

"That wasn't Globke you talked to. That was the facsimile of Globke. Transparanoia markets facsimiles. Everybody under contract has his or her facsimile. It's one of the terms in the standard contract. Once you sign the contract, you're obliged to live up to the terms. This is basic to a sound contractual relationship. At this precise moment in duplicate time, Bucky Wunderlick is having his toenails clipped in the Waldorf Towers. You've been conducting an interview with his facsimile."

I could see myself reflected in his glasses as I rose from my bowl-shaped chair and moved slowly backward toward the door. He raised an arm in shaggy homage.

"Peace."

"War."

5

THE ROOM'S TENSIONS were suitable to few enterprises besides my own, that of testing the depths of silence. Or one's willingness to be silent. Or one's fear of this willingness.

The snow turned brown on the window ledge. There was soup to eat when the old stove worked. Things functioned sporadically; other things functioned all the time but never to full effect. Through large parts of many nights I sat with Opel's coat around my shoulders. The little radio made its noises, fierce as a baby, never listening to itself. This was America's mechanical voice, its doll voice, coughing out slogans into the dawn, testing itself in the event of emergency, station after station fading away in the suffering breath of the national anthem. The firemen stayed in the firehouse.

I heard a noise in the hall and put my head out the door. He was there, sitting on the top step, Fenig again, peering down at me through the dimness.

"I couldn't write," he said. "I got started on a science-fiction thing but it bogged down in the early stages. I tried to walk it out. You know, pace it out. Sometimes it helps, a simple thing like walking up and down a room. When the inspiration peters out, I get off my duff and start pacing. I pace certain ways, depending on the situation. This time I was pacing five steps north, around, eight steps southeast, over to starting point, five steps north again. It sounds stupid but it works. Do something over and over and soon little irregularities show up in the routine. Unconscious, unbidden. This is when you know you're back in business. Come on up. I'll show you my place."

His room was sparsely furnished. It was dominated by an enormous trunk, balding with age, fitted out with huge rusty buckles and other types of metalwork. A rolled-up carpet lay against a wall. Fenig's typewriter was set on a small metal table with wheels. The shade on a nearby lamp had a cup-and-saucer motif.

"This is where I live and work," he said.

This was my first good look at Fenig. Because of the hood, his nose seemed larger perhaps than it really was, and since there is a sense of tragic destiny associated with people who have large noses, Fenig in his sweat shirt made me think of a gym teacher standing in a rainy playground while kids slash laughingly at his arms with improvised knives. We sat in old wooden chairs; on each one, several layers of paint were easily distinguishable in the manner of geological strata. Fenig himself appeared well kept, his clothes neat and recently laundered.

"Nobody knows me from shit," he said. "But I'm a two-time Laszlo Piatakoff Murder Mystery Award nominee. My one-acters get produced without exception at a very hip agricultural college in Arkansas. I'm in my middle years but I'm going stronger than ever. I've been anthologized in hard cover, paperback and goddamn vellum. I know the writer's market like few people know it. The market is a strange thing, almost a living organism. It changes, it palpitates, it grows, it excretes. It sucks things in and then spews them up. It's a living wheel that turns and crackles. The market accepts and rejects. It loves and kills."

Light entered mildly, the only wage a northern winter pays to moderation. A corner of the room began to shimmer, the sun raising dust in uncertain columns, and I realized I was still wearing Opel's coat. Fenig in his cotton-acrylic hood. Wunderlick tucked in at the waist, baring his bony wrists.

"There's a woman lives downstairs," he said. "First floor. Micklewhite. She's got a kid about twenty, deformed and retarded. He was born with something wrong with his skull. It's soft for some reason. His head is full of dents and funny little configurations. His family was ashamed and they never did anything. They just kept him in the room. Now the father's dead and the mother's nutty and the kid is still in the room with his pliable head. He can't talk or dress himself or anything. I don't know if he can even crawl. I've never seen him myself. She doesn't exhibit him around. But she told me everything. Micklewhite and her all-American boy. I've put him in four stories, sight unseen."

The radiator was similar to the one in the room below, a tall stooped object standing in a corner, wholly reconcilable with its surroundings or lack of them, nice to look at and even listen to, the kind of radiator that has a metal receptacle hooked to its back for the purpose of holding water and moistening the air. Our matching radiators. Something to water once in a while.

"Fame," he said. "It won't happen. But if it does happen. But it won't happen. But if it does. But it won't."

The building was pounded by shock waves from an explosion at a construction site nearby. I watched Fenig's jowls quiver a bit, all the loose skin on his face agitated by the tremor, a disquiet at the center of his neatness and calm. There was no sign of a radio, telephone or television set.

"I met Laszlo Piatakoff at a Baskerville Society dinner thing at the Hilton."

"Who is he?" I said.

"Laszlo Piatakoff is the Marjorie Pace Kimball of murder mystery. That's no exaggeration."

Down on the street someone was using a hammer. The sound was vibrant, accompanied by liquid echoes, and soon it was joined by the sound of another hammer, maybe a block away, a thick ripple to each granulating blow, probably Bond Street. The heavier of the two sounds was the more distant, and together they formed a slowly spreading wake, one of time, silence and reverberation, each of these flowing through the others, softening the petrified air, until finally one hammer was rested, and the other grew brutal.

"Everybody knows the thing about an infinite number of monkeys," Fenig said. "An infinite number of monkeys is put to work at an infinite number of typewriters and eventually one of them reproduces a great work of literature. In what language I don't know. But what about an infinite number of writers in an infinite number of cages? Would they make one monkey sound? One genuine chimp noise? Would they eventually swing by their toes from an infinite number of monkey bars? Would they shit monkey shit? It's academic, you say. You may be right. I don't know. One thing I do know. It's all a question of being in the right place at the right time. Knowing the market. Spotting its fluctuations. Measuring its temperament. I've written millions of words. Every one of them is in that trunk."

When I went downstairs I had to content myself with fashioning an impersonation of sleep, eyes closed, body lax, a studied evenness to my breathing. This, in the end, became tiring, and I ate some food and then sat by the window. The air carried a dismal stench, some kind of earth gas released by the detonations. I closed my eyes again. When I opened them it was well into evening. The room behind me was dark. I thought of opening the window and shouting:

"Fire! Hey, fire!"

The great doors of the firehouse would slowly come open. I'd get a glimpse of the big machine, fire-engine red, rigged with shiny appliances. Then tiny men in black booties would appear, edging out onto the sidewalk, lifting their beady eyes to my window.

"Fire!" I'd shout. "Hey, fire, fire!"

One small man would take several steps forward, moving into the light shed by a streetlamp. He'd tug at his booties for a second. Then he'd look back up at my window.

"Water," he would say, barely above a whisper.

A moment would pass and then his little comrades,

standing all around him now, would commence whispering, as if by prearranged signal:

"Water, water, water, water, water."

Finally all the tiny men would return to the firehouse and the vaulted doors would slowly close behind them.

6

A TELEPHONE that's disconnected, deprived of its sources, becomes in time an intriguing piece of sculpture. The business normally transacted is more than numbed within the phone's limp ganglia; it is made eternally irrelevant. Beyond the reach of shrill necessities the dead phone disinters another source of power. The fact that it will not speak (although made to speak, made for no other reason) enables us to see it in a new way, as an object rather than an instrument, an object possessing a kind of historical mystery. The phone has made a descent to total dumbness, and so becomes beautiful.

Opel's phone was out of order and Azarian came down without calling and was waiting for me in the hall, numbed by cold, when I got back from Thirteenth Street, where I'd gone to buy some clothes. He stood against the mailboxes, arms strait-jacketed in crushed velvet. Somehow he managed to invest the simple act of sniffling with an element of gravest accusation. I led him upstairs. Without uncrossing his arms from his chest, he dropped into a chair.

"The apocalyptic crotch himself."

"Don't be funny," he said. "Do that one thing for me, Bucky. Avoid all funny stuff. I'm cold and tired. I need to be talked to seriously. Jet lag, fear, anxiety, depression. You know my history."

"Want some cocoa? Good and hot."

"Sure, yeah, okay."

"I don't have any."

"I thought you were with Opel Hampson in Morocco."

"Is she in Morocco?" I said.

"Globke finally told me you were here."

"How about hot tea? Steaming hot Lipton's tea. Fresh from the grocer's shelf."

"Do you have any?"

"No."

"Frankly I wasn't knocked out by grief when you left, Bucky. But I was wrong. We kind of need you. The last year or so I've been in a state of deep fear nearly one hundred per cent of the time. All kinds of fears of this and that. Mostly unexplained fears. When you left the group I frankly expected the anxieties to lift like a fog. But I was wrong. I'm more afraid than ever. All the tremendous tensions you created with your presence have gotten even worse now that you're gone. I'm afraid all the time."

"Afraid of what?"

"You know my history," Azarian said. "Fears, anxieties, apprehensions, dreads, terrors, cowerings and panics. Don't ask me afraid of what. Afraid of everything, I guess. Everything, nothing, something, anything. I came east for a reason. Really two reasons. Both pretty scary."

"Tell me."

"First I want to know your intentions. I feel I have a

right to that. The band's in flux. Before I can take any definite action and relieve my mind of some of the fear, I have to know whether or not you're thinking about returning. Some idea of your state of mind would be a great help to me at this point. They thought you'd been murdered. Dodge actually thought that. I told him he was crazy. So we talked to Globke to get some kind of idea. We talked to him together. Then we talked to him one by one along the line at different stages. He didn't tell us anything definite till last night. So I came in from Phoenix. Rotten shitty flight. Dodge's mother's been trying to contact you. She's some kind of whatever-you-call-them. Beyond the grave. See, Dodge told her you were dead. So she tried to contact you."

"Any luck?"

"She got your brother, she said. Did you ever have a brother?"

"No."

"That's what Dodge told her. Weird fucking woman."

"I'm kind of busy," I said. "If you could tell me what you want."

"Busy doing what? What could you be doing in a place like this that you could call busy?"

"Tell me what you want," I said.

"I want to know your intentions. I want to know if you're coming back, and when, and in what exact role. In what capacity. Let's face it, you haven't done anything new in a long time and pressure's been building up over that fact and in the meantime I'm ready to go into a studio with material I've been working on for about the last two years that we've never recorded. I'm ready for a whole lot of things. But I can't just go ahead. I'm tied down by prearrangements, by clauses, by small print, by multiple deals and counterdeals. Everything's locked up tight. So this is the necessary first step. Finding out your intentions."

"I have no intentions."

"You do so have intentions. Everybody has intentions. Looks like I was right about you."

"In what way?"

"I told them you cracked up," he said. "Dodge was running around with the murder story. They all believed him. I told them you just ran off to hide. You cracked up. You couldn't take it anymore and you went off to Morocco to hide. I told them that."

"You were mistaken."

"Dodge said Bucky's not the type. Last man to crack'll be Bucky. We'll all fall apart but not him. Well, bullshit, they were wrong. I saw what happened in the lounge in that airport, wherever we were, Denver, just before the Astrodome riot."

"What happened?" I said.

"I saw what happened."

"What happened?"

"I didn't tell anybody because I figured it was your own private business. I didn't even tell them after you disappeared and they were going around believing you'd been murdered. You cracked up pure and simple. I told them that much but nothing else."

"What happened?" I said.

"It caught my eye in all that crush just before we boarded. You were on your knees making faces at some old woman in a wheelchair. I knew it wasn't a joke. It was too unreal for that. You were sweating and babbling and making incredible unreal faces at the old woman. I've never seen anyone sweating the way you were. Laughing and babbling and down on your knees. Laughing-crying. I'll never forget it. A few other people saw it too but nobody knew how to react. It was too unreal. And besides you were in tears. So nobody knew what was what. There was no reality. There was no way to know what to do. Then somebody wheeled the old lady away and you got up and it was over."

"Strange."

"You hadn't said more than five words in about a week and a half, Bucky. I mean the whole grinding insanity of the tour. I mean the incredible sick aspects of it. I mean the whole morbid fantasy. This could smash anybody into little pieces. And being who you were, of course. That whole other myth. Who you were and what you represented. That particular inhuman pressure. When I first saw you on the floor like that, it didn't really seem that unusual. I knew it wasn't a joke but I didn't think it was serious either. I mean that's the tour. That's what happens on the tour."

"Strange," I said.

Azarian's sadness filled the space between us. He leaned forward in the chair now, exploring my eyes, trying in his intensity to make me remember, to make me see my own face, as if this remembering could be a clean breeze through his sadness. He clenched both fists, lined them up against his lips and blew heat and energy into the resulting tunnel.

"That brings us to reason number two why I'm here," he said. "Happy Valley Farm Commune is holding something I'm willing to lay out money for. I represent certain interests. These interests happen to know you're in touch with Happy Valley. So they're making the offer to you through me."

"Make your offers to the people directly involved. I don't want to know anything about it."

"They're an armed camp. I wouldn't go anywhere near them."

"Your problem, not mine."

"Look, Bucky, you and I know each other a long time. That's why these certain interests want me representing them. It makes sense for you and me to do the business in this particular situation. I don't want to go anywhere near Happy Valley. I just want to bid on the product they're holding. I'll make the offer. You take it from there."

"I don't know the first thing about these people."

"Your people or my people?" he said.

"My so-called people. I don't know anything about them."

"Okay, the group was a rural group that merged with other groups or splinter groups and got hassled everywhere they went and so they kept moving and eventually over the years they ended up in the city, this city, right here, within walking distance, Bucky, walking distance of right here. In other words they're a rural group that came to the city to find peace and contentment."

"What's the thing they're holding?"

"The point is we've got the money to make a strong offer," he said. "People on the Coast. Friends of mine I met in Detroit time before last. They have roots in Detroit, they have roots in Cleveland. Now they're on the Coast. I'm in a state of fear every minute I'm with them. But these people represent an important part of my development. Fear or no fear, I'm in this thing to the end."

"You don't know what the product is, do you?"

"It's a simple enough guess," he said. "The point is we've got backing. We've got resources."

"Tell your people I don't know anything. That's more or less the truth. I'm just a tired old figure of the entertainment world. You know that. Music industry wore me down."

"I'll tell them, Bucky, but they won't listen. In the meantime what's in that bag that you could put on the stove and heat up to get this chill out of my body?"

"A lumber jacket," I said.

"One of those old things with red and black checks?"

"I got it at an army-navy store."

"I wouldn't mind running out to buy one of those. Except I have to be uptown in about half an hour to talk to some record people. Heavy names. Monsters of the industry. Then get my ass out to the airport. But back to what we were talking about originally. I'd like to get some kind of answer before I leave here. What happens next, Bucky? Are you coming back soon? Or do I book studio space and take the band inside?"

"Submit all questions in writing to my personal manager, care of Transparanoia Inc., Rockefeller Center, New York, New York, New York, New York."

7

Opel's belongings were everywhere, objects of an earlier life spent in real places, her past on lonely soil. Hers were possessions resonant with time, a sense of years collected, crystal beads, guitar straps, rosewood stash boxes, hardware catalogues, Mexican candlesticks, simplest of things, every one endowed with the power of her absence, electric yogurt maker, ten-foot hand-knitted scarf. I moved the bed to the center of the room. Sleep seemed more possible here.

Fenig came to visit, saying he was in a coffee-drinking mood. I looked around the room for coffee. I looked everywhere without results. Then I looked for cups. There were no clean cups. All the cups were in the sink, sitting inside each other. I looked around for sugar. I tried to find a clean spoon in the drawer of the small cabinet. The drawer was full of string, buttons and penny postage stamps. I began to sweat, a mean animal odor soaking my clothes. I hunted around for a saucer but there wasn't a single one anywhere, clean or dirty. Fenig liked his coffee black so there was no need to look for cream, milk or half-and-half. Someone shouted in the hall downstairs. I opened the door and we went out and looked over the banister. A man straddled a sample case, waving a brush at us.

"Foreign armless vets of the Second War. A three-dollar sum of money guarantees you selected brushes made by handicapped ex–fighting men. Brushes for home, industry, the car, the toilet. Are you self-employed? Brushes for the self-employed. I'll listen to bids, anybody in the building, two-fifty to start it off and you couldn't believe what that sum of money is capable of buying in the way of a pre-selected industrial brush. Armless in the European and Jap theaters of World War number two. They went and they fought. Their names were Ryan, Bandini, Hogan, Ryan. They stepped ashore in strange lands where they didn't know a soul. This is not stolen merchandise. This is merchandise made and guaranteed by the living maimed of our nation. Iwo Jima, Corregidor, Salerno, Tobruk, Belleau Wood, Bataan, back to Bataan, Iwo Jima, Paris, Norway."

"How many wars are you selling?" Fenig said.

"Dollar seventy-five I'll take. A selected car broom. Keeps your dashboard free of foreign matter. Fits any glove compartment, big or little or money back. Jumping out of troop planes. Hand to hand in the trenches. Loose lips sink ships. Graduating from tail-gunner school. Armless and legless. Can't even salute the flag they died for. Ninety-five cents, I'll come up and get it; a quarter, just roll it down the stairs. Guadalcanal, Burma, espionage, ack-ack. They fought on the sea, in planes and trains, on motorcycles with sidecars, under the water in submarine warfare. A three-dollar brush made by a vet for fifty cents even, plus tax. Seven patriotic colors. I am not a hustler. This is not a brush hustle. They came from places like Pittsburgh, Grand Rapids, San Diego, Alabama. They went and they fought and they got hurt, some of them, pretty bad. Kansas City, Kansas. Kansas City, Missouri. It was war, it was war."

We went back inside. I got on my knees and looked in the cabinet space under the sink for some sign of a coffee can. But what sign? Either the coffee can would be there or it wouldn't. There was no sign involved. I kept at it, determined to conduct an intelligent search. The idea of coffee was overpowering. Finding it and brewing it. Feeling the thick liquid wash down my throat and divide itself into tributaries and attenuated falls. If I could find a clean spoon, the coffee might turn up next. My shirt felt heavy and wet, sticking to my back. There was still hope of locating a trace of sugar somewhere in the room — a lump stuck in the bottom of the box, some brownish fossils to be scraped off the sides of the sugar bowl, assuming the box and sugar bowl existed. Given this or even part of it, I might then find coffee or at least a saucer that might lead to coffee. Signs that serve no purpose are logically meaningless, according to something I'd read once and tried to remember. I had it wrong but that didn't matter. I was votary and dupe of superstition. If I could find the box of sugar, it would lead me to a clean spoon. Spoon secured, named and agreed on, we pursue the formal concept to its inevitable end, which is coffee. The salesman appeared in the doorway.

"Marks, drachmas, rubles, pounds, shillings, yens. I'll take anything and everything. The Swiss franc, the

French franc, the Bulgarian stotinki. Here, take a brush for a free ten-day home trial. At the end of that time, pay me any way you like. Piasters, pesos, kopecks, bolivars, rupees, dongs. I'm a long-time student of world currency and exchange rates. I bet you don't know how many puli in the Afghanistan afghani. I bet you can't guess where the kwacha comes from."

"You're talking about thirty years ago," Fenig said. "These guys are still making brushes?"

There is no need to look for cream, milk or half-and-half (I repeated to myself). Fenig likes his coffee black. There is no need to look for cream, milk or half-and-half.

8

HANES RETURNED one day, minus a few of his soft blond locks, dressed a bit less splendidly than usual. He had few virtues as a messenger but I was convinced Globke's use of him entailed more serious things. A sort of image-gathering. Maybe Hanes as an image of my public. Or Hanes as Wunderlick-in-exile. He leaned back against the edge of the raised bathtub, tapping his boot heel on the ancient enamel.

"What do they want?" I said.

"Here's some data from the seventh floor. They thought it should have your immediate attention."

"What is it?"

"Updated assessments and projections."

"Of what?"

"I don't know," he said. "I just know you're supposed to look at this column, that column and the other column. The projections are on the overleaf. They want you to be aware of the current status of things. Then you have to sign or initial this memorandum and I have to take everything back to the seventh floor."

"Stop kicking the tub."

"There's a story you're either doing a concert in England with Watney or you're making a surprise appearance at one of Watney's concerts in America."

"But I'm deceased. I'm deceased, maimed or in Philadelphia."

"These things aren't mutually exclusive."

"You've been pondering these matters?"

"I believe in death-in-life," Hanes said. "One flows through the other. I mean what else is the meaning of a long plane trip spanning continents? What is a three- or four-thousand-mile journey on a 747 except an example of death-in-life? That's the trip you're taking for us. I mean it was your choice and you chose it. You're dead when we want you dead. Then you land and do a make-believe concert. We put you on and take you off. But it was your choice and you chose it. You could have stayed where you were. Things don't get better just because they get more simple."

"I thought you carried signatures back and forth. That's supposed to be your area of competence."

"I don't do anything," he said. "I'm just here — or there. People use me for whatever they want. It's a way of existing. Everybody has a way and this is mine. It's no better or worse than anybody else's."

His voice was malted milk, pleasant and soporific, an Eastern drawl, but determined to mingle certitude and defeat, as if the first could lead nowhere but to the second. Hanes seemed impatient with the world for not knowing the things he knew. The beauty of surrender. The logic of wistfulness. The old age of youth. As I listened I thought a featureless baggy man was striking me in slow motion with a well-polished stone. I moved to another

43

chair, more supple, nearer the window. Some workers placed a guardrail around an open manhole; one of them attached a danger flag and another began to descend. It was late morning. Hanes gave me a piece of paper, then reassumed his stance at the bathtub. I was completely relaxed, melting into the chair.

"That's the memorandum of intent," he said. "You have to sign it or initial it."

"Whose intent?"

"The seventh floor wants you to read it and sign it."

"Can't be bothered, tell them."

"You won't read it?"

"No," I said.

"Will you sign it then?"

"No."

"How about initialing? Will you initial it? Then I can take it back up to seven and they can process it. Or whatever they do. I don't get to seven very often."

"You didn't bring any cash this time. Why is that, Hanes?"

"They said you've spent it all."

"Funny. That's nearly funny."

"You've spent it all, they said."

"It would take eight men eight lifetimes each to spend the money I've earned."

"What you haven't spent is tied up. You've spent a lot."

"What's tied up mean?"

"It's working. They've put it to work."

"Who exactly?"

"The sixth floor."

"I don't want it working," I said. "I'm the one who works. I want my money to sit quietly. That's my idea of the value of money. While I work and sweat, I want to think of my money resting in a cool steel-paneled room. It's stacked in green stacks, very placid and cool, resting up. I realize this isn't everybody's approach to money. But it's my approach and I like it. I envision luminous green stacks. A stainless-steel room. Hundreds of neat green stacks. I don't like to think of money working. I'm the one who works."

"Except you don't seem to be," Hanes said.

I think I slept then, a shallow drop, one level down. A sound seemed to reach me, murderously well regulated, as of sheets of paper sliding out of a Plexiglas machine. I opened my eyes and Hanes was still there, looking down at me, talking right through my sleep, his world-weary TV voice hovering at perfect modulation.

"I like to masturbate in the men's room on six," he said. "Afternoon is best. They're all drugged from lunch. Sitting in their pastel offices. Droning into the phone. I know I'll never get to that point. Their point. I'd rather be used than use others. It's easy to be used. There's no passion or morality. You're free to be nothing. I read their mail. I look in all the confidential files. When I deliver personal notes from floor to floor, I read them in the stairwell. I feel I'm free to do these things. The only thing that unfrees me is music. The men's room on six. I wouldn't try it on seven. I rarely go to seven. The Glob is moving up there next week. He'll probably take me with him but maybe he won't. He'll leave me where I am. That's probably what'll happen. The underground's come up with a superdrug. Did you hear about that? The news leaves me cold frankly. Music is the final hypnotic. Music puts me just so out of everything. I get taken beyond every reference that indicates who I am or how I behave. Just so out of it. Music is dangerous in so many ways. It's the most dangerous thing in the world."

Late in the day it snowed. The men on the radio went wild with news of heavy snow. They seemed unable to stop talking, station after station, into the night, bulletins, announcements, news specials. Every station was on alert for more news of the snow. Programs were interrupted. Announcers sounded close to insanity, their voice levels soaring. Snow watch. Snowplows. Heavy snow. Snowstorm. Deep snow. Big white snow. These men had never in their lives reported stories so full of documentation. It was snowing in this place and that place. It was piling up. It was drifting across the by-passes and interchanges. Their voices nearly cracked with unprecedented mad lyricism as they gave their authoritative reports. It was real snow and it was falling now, at this identifiable point in time. Motorists, pedestrians, vehicular traffic, suburban thoroughfares, snow emergency routes, snow removal equipment, sanitation crews, salt spreaders, accumulations, bridges and tunnels and airports. Snow was coming down out of the sky. It was falling on the city and on the countryside. Big white snow.

Then it stopped. Everywhere the snow stopped falling. The announcers tried to calm themselves. Their disappointment wasn't easy to conceal. Disaster and its various joys had made them hoarse, brought them close to sobs, and now they had to dig themselves out of this massive ecstasy. It was a letdown for everyone. A pre-recorded church service came on and then there was a knock and Fenig appeared at the door, hooded, carrying two paper cups by their shaky handles, his face framed in rising smoke. It was about midnight. I turned off the radio. The house was quiet and no traffic moved on the street. I was beginning to feel completely awake. Fenig seemed tired, bent forward in a chair, slowly knocking his knees together.

"Good coffee," I said.

"It's not instant. I never drink instant."

"I don't think I have anything in the house to eat in case you're hungry."

"It's not hunger that gnaws at me, Bucky. It's a strange kind of fatigue. I get this way from not working. I can't get any work done. But it's not really fatigue. It's non-fatigue, worse in every way. I've had an unproductive eight hours at the typewriter and I haven't sold a thing in almost two weeks. There's no worse feeling than the feeling you get from being unproductive. I jabbed away at that machine all day and nothing happened. Same few sentences. Where's your sugar?"

"I don't know. Maybe in that cupboard. But I doubt it."

"Never mind, I'll drink it bitter. I threw my sugar away because it had a little shriveled corpse in it. Roach-family type thing. You get any down here?"

"I haven't noticed."

"I've written millions of words," he said. "Every one of them is in that trunk upstairs. I've got copies of everything I've written since the beginning. Do you want to know when the beginning was? Before you were born. I had my first story published before you were born. When were you born, just out of curiosity?"

"A few weeks from now twenty-six years ago."

"I had my first story published before you were born."

"But nothing lately."

47

"But nothing lately and that's what counts. It's really fatiguing. All day at the typewriter to type the same few sentences. Were they mediocre sentences? I frankly don't know the answer to that. My response to that has to be that I honestly and truly do not know. Maybe I'll know tomorrow. Maybe never."

"You haven't been pacing," I said.

"I haven't been pacing."

"At least I haven't noticed."

"I haven't been pacing and that's because it hasn't worked lately. I have to change my routine. I have to make an alteration in my format. These things are tricky things. The market's out there spinning like a big wheel, full of lights and colors and aromas. It's not waiting for me. It doesn't care about me. It ingests human arms and legs and it excretes vulture pus. But I understand that. I'm attuned to that."

"Do you hear anything?"

"No," he said.

"Hear that?"

"It's just the kid. Downstairs. The retarded boy. Micklewhite. Her deformed kid."

"What's he doing?"

"Dreaming."

"I've never heard a sound like that."

"That's the way she says he dreams. That's the sound that comes out when he's having a dream. Good thing it's not too loud."

"You were saying something," I said.

"The big wheel."

"I don't remember that."

"The big wheel's spinning out there, full of lights and bright colors and crazy sounds."

"Right, the market."

"Fame," he said. "It won't happen. But if it does happen. But it won't happen. But if it does. But it won't."

"You never know."

"It won't happen. But if it does."

"What if it does? What then?"

"I'll handle it gracefully. I'll be judicious. I'll adjust to it with caution. I won't let it destroy me. Fame. The perfect word for the phenomenon it describes. Amef. Efam. Mefa."

"When do you sleep?" I said.

"I sleep when sleep is feasible. When it's no longer productive to write. I'm working in a whole new area. I guess that's why it's coming so slow. Pornographic children's literature. But serious. Not some kind of soft-core material in a comic vein. Serious stuff. Filthy, obscene and brutal sex among little kids."

"Is there a market?"

"I think this may be the only untapped field in all of literature. Although you never know for sure. Maybe there's somebody working away right now, trying to pre-empt a corner of the market. Once you pre-empt, you're good for years. Send them bird shit wrapped in cellophane, they'll buy it. So I may be too late. There are people typing away all over the place, trying to wedge themselves into little corners of the market. But to get to your question, the answer is yes. Everything is marketable. If no present market exists for certain material, then a new market automatically develops around the material itself. My own brand of porno kid fiction is pretty specific. It has no adults. It is sexy-brutal in a new kind of way. It panders to the lowest instincts. It is full of cheap thrills. It has elements of primeval fear

49

and terror. It has titless little girls saying bad words. It has an Aristotelian substratum."

"If you know this much about it, why can't you get started?"

"I know too much about it," he said.

"No room for discovery."

"No room for discovery and I spent too much time making and taking notes. My energy is pretty much sapped. But the theme lives in my mind. The central motivating force is there. The thrust is a genuine thrust. Little kids sucking and being sucked, fucking and being fucked. No grownups anywhere in sight. Kids obsessed by their magical abilities and appetites. Kids and only kids. Without grownups there's a purity, I feel. The thing is kept pure. Tremendous sadism in evidence. Really vicious stuff. All rendered in terms of the classical forms of reversal, recognition and the tragic experience. But I'll tell you what the clincher is."

"Okay."

"Their organs are extremely sensitive. Small maybe but developed way beyond our own spigots and drains. I plan to hint that this sensitivity is present in all children. A freshness. An innocence. Kaleidoscopic sex organs. Capable of wild fiery pleasure. What we'd all be capable of if we were as pure and sex-obsessed as these children of mine. They're obsessed beyond belief. I can't wait to start writing. But that's not the real clincher. The real clincher lies in another direction."

"Which direction?"

"I'm trying to remember," he said. "All this coffee I've been drinking is beginning to affect my concentration. We're all junkie dope fiends one way or another. I'm firmly convinced of that. With me it's caffeine. But I don't use instant. I never use instant. I wouldn't drink that stuff for anything. I'd drink tea first and I hate tea. But the clincher is the writing style itself. That's it, that's it. I'm doing it like I'd do a second-grade reader. Simplest style imaginable. Easily understood by any seven-year-old kid. In other words I'm not just writing pornography about kids. I'm writing pornography for kids. A fantastic concept in my opinion. I have no doubt there's enough marginally weird people who'll buy books like this for their own kids. Most people will get the books for themselves, for their cataleptic wives and so on. But there's that book-buying minority that's just weird enough to give their kids pornography for Christmas. I have no doubt of this. I think the son of a bitch'll sell. It's my genre and all I have to do is get it down on paper and I pre-empt a corner of the market. I'd like to bang out five quick genre pieces and market them right away. Then I'll get to work on a novella-length piece. Then I'll start a novel. After that I've got a one-acter I want to do about a stockbroker who moonlights as a pimp. Some writers presume to be men of letters. I'm a man of numbers."

"The boy's dreaming again," I said.

Alone now I listened to the sound from below. It lasted more than a moment this time, part of the room's ambient noise, microlife humming in floor cracks, in the air itself. Maybe nature had become imbecilic here, forcing its pain to find a voice, this moan of interrupted gestation. I had never heard a sound so primal. It expressed the secret feculent menace of a forest or swamp, or of a simple plant arching in kitchen sunlight. There seems a fundamental terror inside things that grow, things that trade chemicals with the air, and this is what the boy's oppressive dreams brought reeking to the surface, the beauty and horror of wordless things. I could almost feel the sound under my feet. In the stillness it seemed extremely near, within the room, a dewclaw's mossy flesh touching my ankle. I put on my lumber jacket (symbol of all that's old and wholesome) and ran some tap water, whatever was available, just to hear another noise. Finally everything was quiet and I went to bed. Fenig began pacing then, three steps east, three west, river to river. I slept for a while, very lightly, my surroundings part of the sleep, shaping it in mounds and squares. With my eyes open now I concentrated on various objects within my field of vision. I could barely make out the two candles standing over the sink. The indistinctness of these objects made them seem denser; they were more forcefully present in the near darkness. I slept deeply then, apprehending only myself as object. It was slightly less dark when I woke up, perhaps four in the morning, the room seeming to tremble in the malarial light of that hour. There was no longer any sound of pacing. I turned on my side. Opel was standing in a corner of the room, barefoot, removing her clothes. I lay there watching her, putting her together in my mind as she performed the small acts my eyes could only serialize. I nearly laughed at the way she lost interest in each item of clothing as she took it off, tossing it on the floor or against the legs of a chair, never watching it go, her hands already engaged in the next expert rejection. Her hair was longer now, scattered over one shoulder and deflected at the point of her breast. She had tanned unevenly and her skin was a mass of rash borders and overlapping seasons. No motion she made seemed less than perfect or other than the only motion possible and I wondered at women in their nakedness, how unpreoccupied they are with it, while men either cringe or trumpet. Sniffling she took a handful of tissues from a suitcase and approached on her toes over the cold floor. I moved back in the little bed, making some room, and raised the covers high for her entrance.

"Dramatic," she said.

"What are you doing here?"

"I live here, creepo."

"But it's cold, Opel. Dead of winter. I was sure you'd sit out the winter in some timeless land."

"I've got business," she said.

9

"THERE'S NOTHING more boring than a well-traveled person."

The old tub was mounted on the bruised feet of an ambiguous creature, possibly an imperialistic lion. Opel batted some suds off her nose. She wallowed in the hour-old foam, occasionally adding hot water, sinking quickly to her neck whenever she felt a chill in the room.

"So you've got nothing to tell me," I said.

"It's boring. Who cares? People who travel a great deal lose their souls at some point. All these lost souls are up there in the ozone. They get emitted from jet aircraft along with the well-known noxious chemicals. There's a soul belt up there. People who travel talk about nothing but travel. Before, during and after. This is the world's worst soap, Bucky. Shit, you come into my apartment and live here and go out shopping and bring back absolute crap in the way of amenities for the body. How's a girl supposed to stay pretty? Least you can do is come rub my back. There's a tremendous inner sort of destructiveness to travel talk in the midst of travel. Also too much travel simply isolates people. It narrows them. It makes them boring."

I decided to walk into the tub, not bothering to take off my clothes. We splashed around for a while. That sort of thing isn't fun for long. Opel stepped out of the tub, dried herself and got into bed. I changed clothes and followed. It was probably late afternoon. I was never sure of time while she was there. Alone I lived in the emergency of minutes, in phases of dim compliance with the mind's turning hand. The room had seasons and I responded to these; it was the only way to evade chaos. I knew the phases. I did not fear the crisis inherent in time because I borrowed order from it, shifting with the systematic light, sitting still in darkness. Now none of this mattered. There was a mind besides my own, closing over the room. All need for phases soon vanished, as did all hope of order. We remained in bed a long time, getting up only when necessary. The bed became a shelter within the room. We saw no reason to undress when getting in or to dress when getting out. No one thing kept us there. We immersed ourselves in love and conversation, favoring the latter, ready to settle for the pastels of sex, these milder pleasures being all we could hope to know in our combined quiescence. We lived in bed as old couples rock on porches, without hurry or need, content to blend into benevolent materials, to become, for instance, wood. Even the weather seemed distant, that hard winter pressing less insistently on the window. Opel talked a great deal, delivering herself of observations, conceits and verities. Her more complex monologues were spiral staircases with no ultimate step, just an attractive patch of surreal sky. Other times she inhabited moods of bottomless gloom. My own talk was spare, consisting mainly of background noise. Each day passed, detached from time, linked to no causal nexus, an accident of form and consolidation. The room was striped in transitional light. Through morning's polar tones we huddled under blankets, opening our bodies only to the dark, babbling all the time, eating limp sandwiches and swilling tea. The bed grew in splendor and it began to seem imperative that we remain there. I chose this moment to leave.

"Dip up some ice cream, will you, Bucky?"

"I've been managing without the refrigerator. But I'll go out and get some if you want."

"What are you doing in that chair?"

"Change of scene."

"Not that it's not good riddance. This bed isn't meant for more than one, unless it's wee folk we're talking about, and even then they'd better lie still."

"Do you need a doctor?" I said.

"What for?"

"Nausea and vomiting. Cramps. Back pains. Body tremors. Fevers. Headaches. Coughing spasms. Severe depression."

"That sounds more like you than me. You're the one who looks on the verge. I take medication for my inner organs, to show them I care whether or not they function. I take medication, Bucky. What do you take? You look on the absolute brink. You're functioning day to day on leftover nervous energy. I take medication. Except when I forget."

"Do you want me to go out for some?"

"Some what?" she said.

"Ice cream."

"Some basic weed to suck up might be nice."

"I'd have to get in touch with Hanes. He'd probably have access to just about anything."

"Not Hanes for now. All the fun's gone out of sexual ambiguity. Hanes was never one of my favorite people anyway. Remember how he was always underfoot? A very snaky boy. Sheer snake. Heavy-lidded reptile eyes. But the real reason I don't like him is because he's hard to forget. Every so often I find myself thinking of Hanes. I hate people I don't like who are hard to forget."

"And you're jealous of his heavy-lidded eyes," I said.

"True."

"You've always wanted heavy-lidded eyes."

"Too true."

"Why did you come back? What kind of business? It's cold here, Opel. You're never happy when it's cold."

"I need money, Bucky. Some people offered me an assignment. I'm taking them up on it."

"Maybe I can arrange for you to have some money. Whatever you need for now."

"No, this is business. I'm here to deal. What I make is mine. There's a package here, right?"

"In that trunk."

"Have you peeked inside?"

"I assume it's dope."

"The package contains a raw sampling of what was described to me as the ultimate drug," she said. "Happy Valley Farm Commune stole this stuff from a research installation out on Long Island. The stuff is new, just been developed, has no trade name. They think it's some kind of massive-strength product. But really massive. A colossal downer. They'll know for sure once they get it tested. Happy Valley's anxious to market the stuff but this is their first dope venture on a large scale and they want to be sure not to fuck things up. They don't want to operate out front either. They prefer to work through intermediaries and cover people and so on. I don't want to sound like a gossip columnist of the underground but people have been whispering about this event for weeks now. The dope was taken from a top-secret installation. U.S. Guv. So people figure it's something vicious, mean and nasty. Something U.S. Guv has been putting together to brainwash gooks or radicals. People are anxious to try it and see. People are agog. They're convening in out-of-the-way places and whispering to each other. They're stopping cars on the street and passing the word. Everybody's anxious to get off on this stuff. If U.S. Guv is involved, the stuff is bound to be a real mind-crusher. Anyway that's the consensus. People are agog. It's the dawning of the age of God knows what."

"Your job is to put the stuff in hollowed-out chocolate bunnies and take a plane to Miami."

"I've advanced," she said. "I'm bargaining agent for Happy Valley. I have bargaining powers. I wheel and deal. I don't just hang around the principal parties trying to win Brownie points. There'll be a courier all right but it won't be me. What happens is we'll take the stuff to wherever Dr. Pepper is located these days. Latest word is Dr. Pepper doesn't travel anymore. There's an obvious risk in going to a registered lab so we go to Pepper. Then I haggle for his services. He tells me what the product's chemical capacities are, whether he can manufacture it in sufficient quantities, how much street value it has. So on, so on, so on. Eventually Happy Valley wants to set up a network of wholesalers, retailers and distributors. But for right now what they need is a technical consultant."

"I've been hearing about Dr. Pepper for years," I said. "But never set eyes on the man."

"Some men are legends in their own time. Dr. Pepper is merely a rumor. He's without a doubt the scientific genius of the underground. But very elusive and very crazy and even wears disguises of various kinds. Happy Valley is almost sure they know where he is. Once the location is verified they'll assign a man to me and he'll come walking up the stairs in order to knock on this very door. I will hand him the product and off we'll go to grandmother's house. When the job's all done I will prepare and submit an expense voucher. This is known as finalizing the details of remuneration. Just so you don't think it's all so smooth, I might mention there are two distinct factions at Happy Valley. Certain amount of dissension. That's one of the reasons the product ended up here. The one thing they agree on is your integrity. The true blue example of your life and work, ha ha. They refuse to come in direct contact with you. They consider it an infringement of the worst sort. They're believe it or not very apologetic about involving you in this thing and only did it as a gesture of homage. They have a quaint sense of theater, like all barbarians."

"Time being you just sit and wait, is that it?"

"I don't speak till I'm spoken to," she said. "I just sprawl out in bed and wait for events to take shape."

"In other words you don't initiate."

"I maintain."

"You maintain while others initiate."

"The operative is the one who initiates."

"And eventually there'll be a transaction."

"It depends on the operative. The operative is also the intermediary. Both of them get their instructions from the comptroller. I just sit here until somebody turns up at the door. A tall laconic man with a scar. No, a hip black business-type, that's what I want. One of those purple Cadillac freaks. Stoned behind the wheel of a bullet-proof limousine with silver and gold brocade upholstery. A slow-motion sprinter, that's what I want, neatly spaced on your better-grade euphoriants. I want to carry a Mark Cross briefcase and travel in a purple Caddy."

"Would Happy Valley have blacks working for them?"

"The boundaries are getting indistinct. You never know. Where you've got profit motive the possibilities are endless. But in other ways the lines are getting thicker and straighter. So you never know."

"This business about privacy. What do you know about that?"

Opel took a long breath, obviously bored by the prospect of delivering an interpretation.

"Happy Valley thinks privacy is the essential freedom this nation, country or republic offered in the beginning. They think you exemplify some old idea of men alone with the land. You stepped out of your legend to pursue personal freedom. There is no freedom, according to them, without privacy. The return of the private man, according to them, is the only way to destroy the notion of mass man. Mass man ruined our freedoms for us. Turning inward will get them back. Revolutionary solitude. Turn inward one and all. Isolate yourself mentally, spiritually and physically, on and on, world without end. Sustain your privacy with aggressive self-defense."

"Killer," I said. "Killer ideas. Heavier than cotton candy. Puts me in the mood to read something. About time I read something. What do you have in the house that I can read?"

"What do you want to read about? People, places or things?"

"Things," I said.

"Why not people, creepo?"

"I'm not very interested in human relationships."

"Get behind some coke, Bucky. Shit, if you're interested in reading about *things,* you might as well take a little sniffy now and again. In the long run that's where thingness lies. I met a track star in Dakar. Australian. There to compete in the games. I don't know what games he meant. He kept saying the games. Here for the games. Compete in the games. He gave me some nothing dope. Whatever athletes use. Zero effect. Stepped on about forty times. This is funny. Let me tell you this. I'm sitting in his room waiting and waiting. The games. Here for the games. Compete in the games. Outside the streets are full of lepers. I'm waiting and waiting and waiting."

She went on with the story. It seemed to take hours. I sat in my chair and Fenig paced his floor. This was a perfectly acceptable sonic environment. It was as though tapes of remixed sounds had been run through a computer to extend their frequency range. There was a consoling remoteness to sound now. It lapped across the room in wave-shaped bands, touching nothing. What was said existed on a plane behind the words themselves. Opel was a lump in the bed. I drifted around the room, returning eventually to the circular chair, happy to dwell in the syntonic dome of well-engineered voices.

"I don't guess you care to hear about the galvanized

61

tank under the choir loft. Back home's what I'm talking about as a matter of fact."

"Tell me about West Africa," I said. "How would you rate it in terms of its being timeless? Using, say, Yemen as the norm. Give Yemen a mean rating of ten even. Okay, where does that put West Africa?"

"It's too dull to talk about. I only mentioned it in the first place to get my point across. Thingness. If you're interested in things, either take dope or travel to an ancient country. When's the last time you consumed something?"

"The last something I consumed was an animal tranquilizer. That was maybe eleven weeks ago, give or take five or six weeks."

"What was it like?" she said.

"I really don't remember. It was Dodge and me. We were on a hotel roof. We were looking down on the rooftops of the city. Whatever city it was. And I was trying to work out a theory about how you can determine the psychic state of a given society by looking down on its rooftops. Dodge meantime was cackling over this little plastic box he had in his hand."

"It's quiet, isn't it?"

"Yes," I said.

"What's going to happen to all of us?"

"All of who?"

"I thought it was best to go someplace completely different. Everything was over. Nobody even knew what to wear anymore. The music didn't mean the same thing. I used to absolutely disappear in that sound. But then it ended. What do you do when something ends? I thought it best to go away."

"Sure."

"What are you laughing at?" she said.

"I don't know. I really don't."

"Then stop."

"I'm trying — really."

"Go ahead, laugh. Bastard. Laugh at nothing. It helps pass the time."

"I'm trying to stop," I said.

"No, laugh. I want you to."

"Should I laugh or not? I'm trying to stop. But now you're telling me laugh. I can't talk. Wait a minute. It hurts. Should I laugh or shut up? It really hurts."

"Laugh, idiot."

"Okay, it's over now. It's all over. Wait a minute. It's not over. It's starting again. It's coming up from my appendix. It's beginning to hurt some more."

"You were laughing at what I said. Bastard. All I said was the whole thing was over."

"And you were right to go," I said. "It was better than staying."

"All through now? All finished with your private riot?"

"I think so."

"When are you going back to them?" she said.

"Back to them-who?"

"Here it comes. Another five minutes. Choke, choke, sputter. Somebody give him a bedpan to gurgle into."

"No, I'm stopping. It was a flurry left over from the other one. When am I going back to them? I know exactly who you mean. The people. The crowd. The audience. The fans. The followers."

"The public," she said.

"When I have something to go back with. Something or nothing. Nothing takes more time."

She was sitting up now. I reached over the side of the

chair and lifted several tissues out of the box on the floor. I rolled them up and decided to toss them over to Opel because I knew she would clap her hands softly as soon as she realized my intention and I wanted to witness that small gesture of hers, simple prefix to a game of catch, the mildest of handclaps transformed to a radiant act of grace by the beauty of the child reconstructed in the gesture. After the toss and catch we rested a while, allowing our brief symmetry to decompose.

"I don't guess you care to hear about my piano teacher's biblical sky. This is down-home regional material you can't get just anywheres."

"Hardly hear your voice."

"I'm under the covers again."

"Is that you?" I said. "I thought it was me. I've been sitting here thinking that mound was me. Or that mound had me under it."

"How could you think that? You're there and I'm here. You're the chair. I'm the bed."

"I knew you were there but then I forgot. I knew earlier. Opel Hampson, I thought. It's her and she's there. But then I somehow forgot."

"Maybe you'd better get back over here. Or maybe if I uncovered myself."

"I used to be such a normal boy."

"That was before my time. That was long before I ever set eyes on your celebrated body."

"Were you ever a normal girl?"

"When I was an itty-bitty Baptist my daddy took me to a revival meeting and I made a decision for what's-his-name. That's about as normal a thing as I ever did."

"Were you saved?"

"I was drowned."

"You mean the well-known immersion ritual."

"Immersion's a nice word," she said. "They grabbed me by the neck and threw me in. But that's not when I made the decision. I was *real* young when I made the decision."

"How old were you when you got immersed?"

"I was five or six," she said. "They stood me up alongside the galvanized tank under the choir loft. My piano teacher had painted the River Jordan and a biblical-looking sky on a giant piece of canvas that was set on a makeshift frame behind the galvanized tank. Right nice. Real pretty sight. Then they picked me up by the neck and dunked me. When they got me on my feet again I noticed my dress had floated up around my neck, more or less exposing my entire maidenish bratty six-year-old body to every Southern Baptist thrill-seeker in the vicinity. That moment marked the true beginning of my womanhood."

"Those were the true, real and honest days."

"On Saturday night all the boys used to go up on the railroad bridge and pee down on the passing trains."

"Listen to Fenig," I said. "He's devised a new pattern."

"What's he doing up there?" she said. "It doesn't even sound like pacing. It sounds like he's running around in little circles. I don't think I like having him up there. A man who spends his evenings running in little circles. But I'll tell you what I really don't like. I don't like not liking him. I never used to be this way. I used to have shadings. Now I'm all one thing."

Opel had spent a year at Missouri State Women's College in Delaware, Texas. This fact was all I knew about that year. She'd led a scattered life and saw no reason to

65

elaborate on content. It was enough in her view to present titles, headings and selected prefaces. Her past was such that these did the necessary work. When I met her, in Mexico, she'd just completed two years in New York. All I ever learned about those years was what happened on the very first day. This was a selected preface. The very first day in New York she walked through Bryant Park to get to her hotel. It was December and a man dressed as Santa Claus sat on a bench eating a sandwich. A derelict walked across the park singing, in full voice, "God Rest Ye Merry, Gentlemen." He seemed headed right for the Santa Claus. The Santa Claus watched him for a moment, then got up and began to run away, biting at his sandwich as he fled. Once across Forty-second Street he looked back to see how much distance he'd put between himself and the derelict. Then he ran through traffic on Sixth Avenue and disappeared. Opel gave the derelict a dime and he obligingly exposed himself.

10

SHE WROTE post cards to ten people and I went out to mail them. The cards had been bought in various timeless lands. Palms, mosques and jungle. I walked down the Bowery trying to find a mailbox. I put my hands in my pockets and moved sideways into the wind, trying to slice through, to minimize.

(A corporation word but perfect for our time.)

Maybe that was the answer I needed, the one route back. So simple. To decide to love the age. To stencil myself in its meager design. A mailbox was visible through snow flurries. It was pleasant to drop the little cards in, adding ten names to the great circulatory process of delay. Simple. I might yield to the seductions of void, taking a generation with me into blank climates, far beyond any place we'd been before, chancing endless pain to our children, misbirth and aphasia, all asleep in drool. I had no idea how I might begin. It was important, I knew, never to fear the end of any line I might venture to trace. Important never to alter levels of purpose.

Never to satirize or pursue small ironies or curtsy to the one-handed clapping of the tasteful and humane. I'd have to hand myself over to the structures that defined the time. Float on its clotted oil. Become obese with power and self-loathing. How else to remake myself, to pass the point I'd found, the proportion needed and feared, nothing to nothing. Opel waited in bed, tangled among the sheets, her body labyrinthine in shrouds and pockets of sloppy linen. It was an evil thing to consider, allying myself with the barest parts of mass awareness, land policed by the king's linguists, by technicians in death-system control, corporate disease consultants, profiteers of the fetus industry. I wondered whether I'd need a new following or whether the old would simply rearrange itself to accommodate my second coming. This was possibly the most interesting aspect of the problem. But either way I'd be the epoch's barren hero, a man who knew the surest way to minimize.

"I hated to get rid of those cards," Opel said. "They were so beautifully ugly."

"What did they say?"

"They said it's your birthday in four days and would so-and-so come over for a little ether and muscatel."

"Thanks for letting me know."

"I thought you'd read them."

"I looked at the pictures."

"You see, I thought you'd read them and that your failure to comment was an indication of tacit approval. That's what I frankly and sincerely thought as a matter of fact. Anyway they'll be here in four days. It'll be the last party. Assuming everybody's still at the addresses the cards were mailed to."

"Nobody's coming here in four days," I said.

"Why not?"

"I didn't mail the cards."

"Lie," she said. "I caught you in a lie. You hadn't read the cards so there was no reason not to mail them."

"I lied when I said I hadn't read them. But I'm telling the truth now. I read them. But I didn't mail them."

"You're too messed up to read."

"Okay, it's true I hadn't read them. But I suspected what was written on them. So I didn't mail them."

"Not even remotely convincing."

"I gave them away. There was a beggar over near Stanton Street. I gave him the post cards to sell for black bread and soup. The beggar then revealed himself to be a sixteenth-century English saint. Nigel of Chelsea. He gave me his credit card to use for thirty days without fear of criminal prosecution."

"I always know when you're lying regardless of what comes out of your mouth. You become very still. And your eyes get hard. You try to overpower the person you're lying to. When I lie I try to slip past like a little stream. But you, you're like Easter Island."

"Tell me who's showing up for the last party."

"Oh, everybody."

"Can you give me an example?"

"Oh, you know, everybody."

"Bright lights of the past. Is that it?"

"The neon creepies."

"Opel, shit."

"They're just folks, Bucky."

I slept with my head somewhere under her arm. When I woke up it was nearly dark. Opel never appeared peaceful in sleep. There were other times, certain expressions she made, when I could see exactly what she'd looked like at the age of ten; this funny child smiled out from the middle of her face. But in sleep she was faintly angry, twice her true age, laboring through dreams and panic, a menopausal line coursing down her jaw. Sleep drained her of impulsiveness and failed to replace it with some approximation of its opposite, serenity or resignation. Opel did not rest easily. She was a bed-fighter, kicking, angling for position, making carnivorous noises. The trance was a kindlier state for her. In the past we'd cruised together into various distorted modes and she never failed to evolve security from a chemical's endless suburbs. She belonged dead center in that ferocious calm; it steadied her as sleep never could. I woke her up now and made love with whatever strength I could summon, whatever bruising resolution, a fresh edge to body and mind, drawn from that walk in the wind, power-resurgent-now, teased by the feeling I might soon return to the sound outside. Her body gave me back the heat of sleep, responding slowly, no longer greedy in its freedoms, a body rising like bread, her loins poised, tongue at my ear, hand knuckling along my spine, and it was art we sought to shape, a moral form to master commerce, the bodies we were and the danger we needed, that of dredging each other's insufficiencies, touring the deepest holes. We rode an odd moment now, laughter back and forth, her eyes alert to love's delight, an instant only, then down to pelvic business, rack and pinion, the poet's word dropping off the page. Through the day Opel remained in bed, resting up (she said) for her mercantile encounter. I dialed numbers on the dead phone.

"Why is ecology so boring to read about?" she said.

"For the same reason destruction is such fun."

"Old magazines are pretty. Don't you think?"

"Sure, why not."

"This one says Spain is a land of contrast. I'll have to go there soon."

"It may not be timeless enough for you."

"Right now I need contrast. The eye gets tired as hell seeing the same surroundings. That's the second and final justification for travel as a matter of fact. To keep the eye interested."

"What's the first?" I said.

"To become a thing. I told you that."

"But is there any land that isn't a land of contrast?"

"I don't know. But Spain makes an outright claim. If you went somewhere where they didn't make the claim, you'd be taking a big chance. You might get there and find no contrast at all. No, it's definitely Spain. I'm going to Spain."

"Spain," I said into the phone. "Get me the Spain the tourist never sees."

"When are you getting out of here, Bucky? Don't you want to make some sounds? You haven't written anything, you haven't played, you haven't even hummed. What the hell, man."

"What the hell, man."

"You should be playing."

"You should be dealing," I said. "Where's your man? If your man doesn't show up, where are you then? You'll have to go back to Texas and manage your daddy's empire. You want to deal, that's dealing. Why'd you ever leave? Come up here in this freezing gray slush. Hang around in that little bed waiting for some long-time weird geek bureaucrat to drive up in his pimpmobile and knock on your door. It makes no sense."

"Could be you're right. But I know one thing. My eyes need contrast."

"Spain," I said into the phone.

Several days later people of various sorts appeared in the room. Some I knew; others were unknown to me. I sat in the bowl-shaped canvas chair. Opel led the celebrants around me. I nodded, blinked and occasionally touched another's jutting hand. I had little to say but was sure no one would mind. They already knew my voice. It was my presence they were eager to record, the simple picture of man-in-chair, a memory print to trade for other people's time. Slowly the room began to fill. It became obvious the original ten were intent on trebling. People spoke of where they lived, in what shamble of rooms or post-atomic street. Of their health, poor and poorer. Of bands of howling boys abroad in NoHo. Of distant spring on the banks of the East River, stoic pic-nickers watching bodies rise to the surface, braided in weed and pecked by idle fish. Someone mentioned the loft he'd just moved into, a large windy place, floors buckled and humped, no lights without a kite and key. Of teen-age wino communes. Tia Maria modeled (draped) for art students at Cooper Union. Chester Greenlee panhandled on Eighth Street, wearing a Mickey Mouse mask. Miss Mott lived alone on Mott Street, as in the past, called Miss Rivington, she'd lived on Rivington Street, and on Canal Street as Miss Canal. She was in her late sixties (it was speculated), a collector of Dad's Root

Beer bottles and copies of the *Wall Street Journal*. I took a breath and then another. A man smoked a pipe, sitting with legs jauntily crossed, dressed in patched corduroy. The neon creepies chatted and wept, bad teeth, worse posture.

"This is the last party."

"Look, I'm wearing my forty-dollar chinchilla Luv Glove. It's a gesture. We need gestures today. People's stomachs are shrinking with fear. We need to wear each other's underwear. I issue this edict. Wear each other's underwear. It's a gesture of faith in each other. It's the end of fear."

"Oh God my head. Oh my whole mind. My limbs and extremities. Oh God my hair, my nails, my pores."

"I'm troubled by movie dreams. Glamorous faces appear and disappear. All the great names. I find it troubling for some reason. I wake up fearful and unsettled. The faces are sad. Maybe that's it. The sadness of great fame. The famous movie dead. Dead but not dead. That's why I'm unsettled maybe. Because they're unsettled. Dead but not really dead. Never really dead. The whole concept of movies is so fundamentally Egyptian. Movies are dreams. Pyramids. Great rivers of sleep. The great and the glamorous with their legendary sphinxlike profiles. I wake up trembling."

"This is the last party."

"I was all set to wear my sequined baby-doll nightie from Frederick's of Hollywood and come crashing out of a big freaky birthday cake. But I settled for the Luv Glove. Nobody makes gestures today. We're all scrunched up like piglets being born. Opel, mail me some underwear so I'll feel better. Yours and Bucky's. Lycra, mail Bucky your underwear, one or two things. It's a gesture of faith. People need each other. I issue this edict. A chain letter with underwear enclosed. Everybody who gets the letter mails one pair of underwear to the next name on the list. If nobody breaks the chain, we end up with sixty-four pairs of underwear each. Of and for the people. I'm pro-people. This is a people thing."

"Of course I act like a child. Of course I revert. Of course I'm anal."

"Burnt skin, Opel, use mink oil soap. And your hair looks like an Arab's been chewing on it. Use a comb to style. Use a brush to condition. And rinse with Jell-O, sweetmeat."

I continued to breathe, never before conscious of the effort needed to generate this act. People passed supernaturally across the room, leaving contrails of smoke and scented ash. Others settled around me, moving their lips. All were breathing, sullenly pumping blood, embarked together on a perverse miracle. Our movable parts carried us past the edge of every deathly metaphysic. Our organs, lifted from our bodies, plucked out with silver pincers and left laboring on bright Tiffany trays, would comprise the finest exhibit of our ability to endure. Euphoric with morphine we'd be wheeled among them, noting proportions and contours, admiring the beauty of what we were. In death, our opened bellies dripping, we'd be placed in refrigerated elevators and sent soundlessly into the earth. Above, our organs would be tagged and stored. Or, if found defective, fed to the poor.

"It's axiomatic that history is a record of events. But what of latent history? We all think we know what happened. But did it really happen? Or did something else happen? Or did nothing happen?"

The pipe-smoking man crossed and uncrossed his legs, a shade of vaudeville in the genealogy of his movements. He banged the pipe into an ashtray, inspected the bowl, blew into the stem, inserted a grimy pipe cleaner. Around him people spaced from birth passed chocolate kisses hand to hand. The pipe-smoking man began to refill his pipe, treating the instrument with appropriate manly endearment.

"I'm Morehouse Professor of Latent History at the Osmond Institute. But I don't occupy the Morehouse Chair. I occupy the Houseman Chair. This professorship deals with events that almost took place, events that definitely took place but remained unseen and unremarked on, like the action of bacteria or the rising and falling of mountain ranges, and events that probably took place but were definitely not chronicled. Potential events are often more important than real events. Real events that go unrecorded are often more important than recorded events, whether real or potential. At one time sixty per cent of the population of black Africa was white. We have tools and femurs. But we're not sure what happened to this blue-eyed race. Were they wiped out by wars and disease? Did they sail away in long wooden ships? We're still sifting materials at the Homer Richmond Blount Memorial Wing of the Institute and we hope to have some answers very soon. One of the major thrusts of latent history is to avoid a narrow purview. We're presently assembling evidence about the French Revolution indicating that a dissident faction of the sans-culottes used to assemble secretly under cover of dark for the sole purpose of wearing culottes. They'd strut around all night in foppish knee breeches. An orgy of strutting and posturing. At daybreak they'd get into tight-fitting pantaloons and go back to their revolutionary activities. History is never clean. In some cases less happened than we suspect. In other cases we merely suspect that less happened. It's axiomatic that people in the Middle Ages went to bed early. We're studying this to learn what effect it had on the Hundred Years' War dragging on for as long as it did. Latent history never tells us where we stand in the sweep of events but rather how we can get out of the way. I myself am currently doing a paper proving that the Reformation, as such, never took place. The Counter Reformation was a response to something that never happened, as such. The Nile once flowed into the Amazon. We have sediment to prove it. What dreams did it carry? How much of the blood and poetic impulse of all of us? These are among our central concerns at the Institute."

Lloyd Boyd stood in the doorway, then spotted me and came over. Lloyd was an actor who'd recently served time on a charge of reckless endangerment. Since his release he'd been living in Grand Central Station, sleeping on benches or in the doorways of clam bars. He told me he tried to think of Grand Central Station as his apartment. One room but a nice size. High ceiling. Nice big window. Marble floor. Centrally located, always important for an actor making the rounds. A little bit noisy and could be more heat. But the high ceiling made up for everything.

"I got depressed so I took an antidepressant."

"As who wouldn't?"

Lycra Spandex lived with her mother and sister in Lefrak City. I didn't know where Vegemato lived. Lynn Forney lived with Notorious Nora and the Seventh Fleet on Avenue B. Jerry Dane lived in an East German Vopo greatcoat. Tia Maria used to live in a city bus abandoned under the West Side Highway but truck drivers on their way to the meat terminals used to ram the bus for fun, sometimes stopping just long enough to rape Tia Maria, more or less, and finally she moved into a storefront church presided over by a man who wore spats and claimed to be a direct descendent of Mohammed. I closed my eyes a moment, aware of a woman's voice depositing names at my feet.

"Bucky, this is Zenko Alataki, who happens to be Axel Gregg the documentary film–maker's brother-in-law, and I'm Axel's sister Lillian, Zenko's wife, Lillian Alataki. My husband's just up from northwest Mexico to raise some money for the earthquake he's been working on down there. Just make sure you don't call it art. It's not art. It's back to before art. Fire-building and the fingering of testicles. The wonder of pre-information is that men perceived the earth and themselves actually in the process of changing. Zenko's been trying to create pressure along a fault with a series of very delicate TNT explosions. Just a few more in the right places and he'll have his small quake. The greatest work of art ever achieved. Except don't call it art."

"Is this true?"

"Why not?" Zenko said. "The continents ride on plates. The crust shifts, which causes breaks or faults. The beauty of a man-made fracture is that you can photograph the adjacent surface. Place objects on the surface and take aerial photographs of the objects toppling. I call this a kinetic shiver. Objects toppling. Objects being swallowed up. If society wasn't so obsessed with false values, I would be permitted to use live animals in my shivers. Sheep, goats, some rabbits. Earthquake technology enables man to give back to the earth. Goats being swallowed up would make a perfect shiver. It's an act of sacrificial love. We give back. The earth takes and is greener. How much do you weigh?"

"Is this the first shiver you've worked on?"

"This is the world's first shiver," he said. "I'm being prudent but bold. Life-serving destruction is always bold. How much do you weigh? Have you noticed what a very emaciated group this is? It's as though you're all disappearing before my eyes."

Opel went to bed fairly early in the evening. People crawled over and around her, and a few of the more forlorn simply remained at her sides in little ribbons of woe. Diane Bowie took a teddy bear with her into the bathroom. Voices seemed to burn slightly. People bit the tips off chocolate kisses, bad teeth, smudged fingers, horrible posture. Winona Barry said she'd advertised her sewing skills in a West Village newspaper. A man called, wanting a nun's habit and crotchless riding pants. They bargained in spare phrases. "Extra for perversion." "Money no object." "Extra for satiny underthings." "Do a sensitive job." "Extra for the hole in the riding pants." "I'll send plenty more business your way." Miss Mott tried to dial the time on Opel's phone.

"My sister has a new fella," Lycra Spandex said. "He's a detective with the safe, loft and truck squad. He took one look at me and nearly gagged. How do I tell a fella like that about the childhood I spent dreaming of lash curlers, mascara, highlighters and toners? Can I explain to a plainclothes man about gauzy blouses, long flared skirts, superbitchy underwear, chokers, earrings, pins and clips? He's a plainclothes man. He wouldn't understand, would he? Do I dare tell him what it means to wear eye shadow and have skin that's rose-petal soft? All my life all I've ever wanted was to be two people. Marge and Gower Champion. Alternating day to day. Can I confide in this detective? Can I explain about the whole Fox Movietone era and those girls in tutus jumping over the sawhorses? This detective spent his entire adolescence hitting other kids with bicycle chains. I'm supposed to tell him about my sheer pantyhose that do away with crotch sag? Sorry but I won't play that game. I know what's best for Lycra Spandex. Lycra Spandex does not have to kowtow to authority figures, even when they're with the police department of the city of New York, even when they're with the safe, loft and truck squad. If the son of a bitch is so great, why doesn't he get me a decent loft to live in, or a safe where I can keep my crappy jewelry, or a fucking truck that I can drive over a cliff?"

A tall pale girl stood near my chair. Her red hair was in pigtails and she wore paint-streaked jeans and a T-shirt with a hole in the middle. I leaned over and touched her arm. Therefore I am. She turned and I put my mouth to her navel. This made her laugh and twist a bit. Softly her thumbs browsed about my ears. Her navel was lint-free, abnormally large, an inner moon of convolutions and repose. There was no reason to wonder who she was or how that level moment was rounded by her hands.

"Name's James," someone said. "Heard and enjoyed your stuff. Third album's a landmark work. Stunning album. Noise and screaming and babble-babble. Heard all your albums and all your singles and liked them all and that comes from someone who's kind of famous in his own right except nobody knows it. Mylon and I. I'm a friend of Mylon's. We live in the same piss-hole building. I gather you're laying back. Understandable. There's nothing to paint and nothing to write and nothing to film and nothing to sing about and nothing to make love to. But your sound comes out of the radio all the time. Stunning sound. Amazing when you think about it how your sound is big even out there in the sticks and boondocks where I come from originally, the absolute sticks, the deep boonies, where it's unlike a big city where people can absorb that kind of sound. Your second LP is killer too but I think number three's the landmark work."

Mylon Ware stood in a corner talking to no one. He was a folk singer from western Canada, a lean bleak man with strange eyes. His second winter in New York he killed and ate his dog to keep from starving. People had offered him food and urged him to go on welfare but he took nothing, listened to no one, said not a word. The dog was a German shepherd, bought for protection, and very hard to kill. Mylon began by using the long bar that was part of his police lock. The first blow wasn't severe or direct enough and the bar proved too long a weapon for the kind of struggle that followed. However it was useful for holding off the dog while Mylon maneuvered with his hunting knife, also bought for protection. It took him fifteen minutes to kill the animal. When it was over, almost nothing in the small apartment stood in the same place or was free of blood. Mylon cut the dog up and over a period of four days cooked and ate whatever seemed edible.

"This is the last party."

"The first act is better in the New York production. The second act is better in the London production."

"Kiss."

"This is my vision. Everybody in the whole world wearing each other's underwear. Whole nations exchanging underwear. China doing Egypt's laundry. Big strong Turks wearing panties from Scarsdale. A people thing. I'm pro-people all the way. It would help us so much. I see it in my mind's eye. Special fourth-class rates for underwear. Cargo ships full of underwear plying the trade routes. This is my vision. Underwear chain letters. World peace through underwear."

"I admit I whimper. I admit I'm fantastically infantile most of the time. I admit I want to sit on the floor and say ma-ma, da-da, na-na."

"For a Filipino she's practically statuesque."

"Winona's little baby is the shittingest little baby you'll ever want to see. That little baby should have its own agent. That baby has a talent no other baby will ever come close to. I told Winona get on the phone to William Morris. That little baby should have an agent."

"This is the last party. Pass it on."

"I'll tell you how I'm shooting this picture. I'm shooting it beautifully. That's how I'm shooting it."

"This is the last party."

"I'm selling comic books on Fourth Avenue. It's a living, right? Kids come in. College boys with the hair, the clothes, the skin. I sell them old comics. I sell them glossies of Bonita Granville and King Kong. They don't call it a living for nothing. It's a living. I live. There's worse could happen. I at least live. It's a living. I make a living."

"This is the last party. Pass it on."

"The Self is inside the Other. Motion is the guiding mind of the solar community."

"Happy Valley's into violence now."

"Kiss."

I thought of all the inner organs in the room, considered apart from the people they belonged to. For that moment of thought we seemed a convocation of martyrs, visible behind our skin. The room was a cell in a mystical painting, full of divine kidneys, lungs aloft in smoke, entrails gleaming, bladders simmering in painless fire. This was a madman's truth, to paint us as sacs and flaming lariats, nearly godly in our light, perishable but never ending. I watched the pale girl touch her voluptuous navel. One by one, repacked in sallow cases, we all resumed our breathing.

11

In sleep I opened an unnumbered door and found the sea. It was wide and still, veneered in delirious silver. Someone I knew was walking along a road that went down a hill toward some houses. The heat was brilliant. Vindictive light burned into the stone of all the small houses chalked near the sea. I heard voices and thought I saw people at the door.

Opel toasted frankfurter buns for breakfast or whatever meal it was. She held the buns on a fork over the burner, toasting the insides of the buns intended for me, the outsides of those intended for her. Each of us thought the other strange for his/her preference. She spread strawberry jam on the buns and brought everything to bed with her.

"I wish we had real strawberries," she said. "Big whole strawberries to look at and eventually eat."

"Live strawberries instead of strawberries on tape."

"I remember traveling literally about six thousand miles in four consecutive flights and then getting to somebody's house I knew and they were eating strawberries and I just sat there and looked at these strawberries sitting in sugar in the middle of the table and it was inconceivable, it was like returning from the land of the dead. They lived, the strawberries lived. I could look right into them. I understood what strawberries really are, not that I could put it in words. They were inconceivably beautiful, so rich and plump and alive, actually glowing from within. Of course I was probably stoned on something."

"Who were you talking to at the door?"

"I thought you were asleep."

"I was asleep but I wasn't fast asleep. Somebody was at the door and the two of you talked about something. It wasn't Fenig because I know Fenig's voice. It wasn't the woman downstairs because it was a man. So I surmise one thing. It was the man you've been waiting for. The courier. Is that who it was?"

"It was the man," she said.

"Good news or bad?"

"Dr. Pepper is not where he's supposed to be. But they expect to reach him in forty-eight hours. I don't know why it's forty-eight hours. Why not forty-seven or fifty-three? Anyway I'm to be ready to leave at a moment's notice as of tomorrow night. I told him I've been ready for days. He expressed the hope we'd function well together."

"Glad it's finally under way?"

"Except one thing bothers me. He wasn't what I'd hoped to get. I thought he'd resemble some lower-echelon A-and-R type like from Motown. Bronzed glasses, wispy beard, that hunched-over funky walk. I expected pure funk, you know? Someone who's spent his whole life dealing merchandise of one kind or another."

"What did you get?"

"I got Hanes," she said.

"Goddamn, that voice I heard. Hanes. On one level I knew it was him. You didn't tell me Globke was involved in this."

"He's not, Bucky. Hanes is free-lancing. It's not surprising it's him really. There are so many people we know in common. If you put all the names on paper and draw lines back and forth, it would probably be very logical that Hanes would be the one to show up at my door. Anyway seeing him gave me an idea. It involves a surprise for you. Your birthday present in fact. Belated maybe but a stroke of true bitch genius."

"Can't wait."

"A gift that's rich with I don't know what."

"Hanes is a human blotter," I said. "I don't like it when people like that get involved in this kind of enterprise. He's very limp. You could pick him up, use him as a blotter and throw him away. Submissiveness and paradox. He'd just as soon do business with the police."

"I'm nice and settled," she said. "Go toast more bread."

It was getting dark. I left all four burners on. We finished the buns and Opel lay in bed eating jam off the blunt edge of the knife. The power of her immobility was beginning to fade. Departure was implicit in everything she did now. Until Hanes appeared at the door, Opel's presence had been immense; she'd reigned in that bed like a bloated Creole queen of the swampland, giddy with magic, wallowing in the sensual pre-eminence of her own stink. Opel had stolen my immobility. I had been motionless as salt. People had swirled around me and I had plotted changes in the weather, gradations of light and silence. I had centered myself, learning of the existence of an interior motion, a shift in levels from isolation to solitude to wordlessness to immobility. When Opel occupied that center I became the thing that swirled.

"Maybe I'll be going back out," I said.

"Out on tour? What with?"

"I'm not sure yet. In fact I've no idea at all. But I'm thinking of getting back out. That's the important thing. Time to stop looking at the wall. You were right. Time to get out."

"Why not work on new material and let it go at that? Why go on tour?"

"That's got to be part of it. I'm not sure why. Maybe I just want the contact. You can't reach extremes by working in a studio. I want to reach extremes. It's like a passage from suicide to murder. I'd been all worked out and fucked over and grabbed at. Suicide was nearer to me than my own big toe. It was the natural ending. I mean it was right there. No one would have been surprised or shocked. I really think it was expected of me. If I hadn't left the tour, one way or another it would have happened. A soft papery collapse. Even after I left, the thing was right there looking me in the face. But now I think I'm out of that. I want to return but in a different way. New extremities. It's like a passage from suicide to murder."

"I'm not sure I get it, Bucky."

"It's too evil for a mere dealer like yourself."

"You want to return with a whole new thing. But what thing? You can scream ugly lyrics and throw rattlesnakes at the audience. Is that the general idea? You can sing love songs to the Pentagon."

"Nothing political," I said.

86

"There's nothing out there but a dull sort of horror. You can't just churn it up into your own fresh mixture. Hero, rogue and symbol that you are."

"Maybe I don't want to churn it up at all. Maybe I want to make it even duller and more horrible. I don't know. One thing's sure. I can't go out there and sing pretty lyrics or striking lyrics and I can't go out there and make new and louder and more controversial sounds. I've done all that. More of that would be just what it says — more of the same. Maybe what I want is less. To become the least of what I was."

"Sure, the beast is loose, least is best. But who's the beast in this case? Be careful you don't twist your own neat lyric. Of course that may be exactly your intention. In which case I look on with interest. Ready as a matter of fact to offer whatever aid and comfort you feel you need. Hell, man, we're old friends."

"Old and true," I said.

"Old, true and lasting."

"No doubt about it."

"Absolutely."

"Sure as shit."

I turned off the burners and stood near the window. Steam whistled distantly in the pipes. I wasn't unhappy being where I was. Things here were not deprived of their emanations. The distances were correct; noise was undisguised; air was allowed to flow without recirculation. But this completeness seemed less than enough to keep me now. I struck a wooden match and put the flame to one of the candles over the sink. Opel pretended to evade this shallow light, sinking deeper into the bed.

"People are getting to be all one thing," she said. "Look

at me, for instance. I used to have shadings. Now I'm all one thing. Civilization by reflex. If we'd been alive in Pavlov's day he could have saved a whole lot of money on dog food. Now take you now. If you want to go back out as a Las Vegas version of what you were, fine with me except I hope you know what it is you're doing. You'll lose the perspective and the edge will crumble and you'll really become the other thing. Maybe it's a natural evolution. You were getting incoherent anyway, album to album, more so all the time. By the end you were making incredible amounts of noise and communicating absolutely nothing. The whole band was all curled up like a burning piece of paper. You know what you did? You embraced the insanity you were telling us about. So maybe it's a natural evolution. You were too much in love with the horror going on because it formed your sound for you and you were fascinated by it as subject matter. It could very well be the natural next step that you crawl out on the stage at the Sands and just sit there in a jockstrap grunting. Ever since I've known you, you've been surrounded by money-grubbing and talk of money and people dealing and operating but that's the last thing you'll ever be corrupted by, money, even if you were literally starving. It's yourself you have to watch out for, that little touch of the antichrist. It happens to be what I like most about you and of course it accounts for your fame and your glory so maybe I'm wrong to even bring it up. But evil is movement toward void and that's where we both agree you're heading. It's your trip. I'd help you get there if I was sure you wanted to go. In my own bitch-genius way I think I've already put a certain teasing idea into circulation, soon to end up on this very doorstep. You have been listening to a panel discussion on a subject yet to be agreed on. Our panelists will now disrobe and paint each other's bodies in colorful native pigments."

Opel's stillness was losing its essential tenor. It was infiltrated by heavy engines, becoming merely a vigil now, that of a lone woman standing in the off-hour calm of a fluorescent tunnel leading to a boarding gate. In candle-flame she seemed almost an after-image, little left of her ascendancy. Again she is reduced to a point in the middle of the sky. On paper one can find her with the aid of a compass and protractor. She is whisperingly civil, seated between an investment banker and a chummy transvestite, thinking ahead to baggage area and customs. Super-freaks are everywhere, smugglers and global dopers contaminating the air lanes, nitroglycerin concealed in their teeth, unripe opium pods surgically sewn under their eyeballs. Slums and revolution on the 747s. She was in rehearsal for departure now. Ever since Hanes. Hanes had stood in the doorway of my Mediterranean dream.

"Places are always what you expect," she said. "That's both the trouble with places and their redeeming feature. I'm certain it wasn't like that in the past. But it sure is that way now. A few places are still different from each other but nowhere do you find something different from your own expectations. Look at post card manufacturers. They take a sleazy tourist-trap lake and try to make it into the canoeing grounds of the gods. But they do such a slick glossy job that you glance at the post card and you know at once this is a shit-filled lake and all the tourists here are either war criminals or people who spit when they laugh. Not that there isn't beauty in such places. That's just it. The whole world is turning into Lafayette Street, the most ugly-beautiful street in New York City. In a way it's nice to get what you expect. It's as though places can be passive just like people. They just sprawl out with their cathedrals and deserts. Passivity is beautiful too. You take what they give you these days and if everything's getting ugly the only thing you can do is try to teach yourself it's beautiful, it's beautiful. Eventually maybe it is. But look at the passivity of Hanes. There's a sexed-out beauty there. Got to admit it, right? Timeless lands. Look at timeless lands. Why do I spend so much time in timeless lands? Because there's no time there, I guess. Because you stop evolving. Because the warm winds polish you like stone. Here where it's cold I develop and become angular and rapidly age. Great Jones, Bond Street, the Bowery. These places are deserts too, just as beautiful and scary as a matter of fact, except too cold for some people. The places where I get coldest are my eyes and my knees. Isn't that a weird number? Eye-muffs and knee-gloves are the obvious answers. Transparanoia might want to get into that. Talk to Globke first thing tomorrow."

I walked around the bed and ended up once more at the window. Opel covered herself to the chin. I had never known exactly what we needed from each other. Maybe it was enough to come and go; we were each other's motion and rest. The telephone sat on four phone books stacked on the floor. One candle burned, the other did not. I exhaled on the window. There was a loud sound in the pipes, the hollowing-out of dank iron. Opel's collection of pennies filled two ice trays in the refrigerator. The bathtub was full of used water. Citing these things to myself was probably an attempt to group the components of a return to order.

"Things evolve just like people and places," she said. "Or to put it another way, people and places are a lot more static than they'd like to believe. Look at me. What have I become in the scheme of human evolution? Luggage. I'm luggage. By choice, inclination and occupation. What am I if I'm not luggage? I open myself up, insert some very costly items and then close up again and get transported to a timeless land. Do you want to know who knows I'm a thing? Customs knows. Customs knows a lot more than we give him credit for. Customs understands the methodology. He knows the way things work. I'm luggage. No doubt about it. Girlskin luggage. But I don't like that word very much. Lug-gudge. Heavy brutish word for a delicate thing like me."

The knife stood in the empty jar, blade up. The unwound clock was on its back in the bottom of the closet, helpless as an insect, legs in the air, winding key partly dislodged. I watched snow come down now, confined in the precise light of streetlamps. There was no wind. The snow dropped straight down, very slowly, asserting itself with the dignity of a country snow, that language of credence and bare trees, milk on the hillsides, old men gigantic in their bootprints. The firehouse doors were closed. A little car went by, yellow, pink, orange and green, no plates visible. When I turned from the window, Opel was dead. The change in the room was unmistakable. I went to her side to touch her once. Her mouth was open slightly. The blanket had slipped to her neck. Very still. Never to be challenged in this particular stillness. There was no expression on her face. Here I am, dead. That was the only thing I could imagine she might be trying to say with her mouth open like that.

This is what I did. I went back to the window and crossed my arms over my chest, wedging my hands in my armpits. This for warmth. I had been brought up to regard death as an irrevocable state. I tried to reconsider this proposition now, to go over the steps one by one, and I wanted to be warm while I did this.

Eventually I unplugged the bathtub, draining it of gray water. I got the broom and swept in a careless manner for about ten minutes. This was panic of such depth it seemed lodged in being itself, my own, a dread of forgetting what I was called or what language I spoke. I put Opel's things away, the few items hanging from chairs or looped over this or that doorknob. I put these away in the closet. After this I spent some time in the bathroom scraping out the soap dish.

This is what else I did. I looked everywhere for change and then went out to find a telephone. Aloud I repeated three sounds: *wun der lick*. Walking south on Broadway (downtown, always down), I repeated these sounds over and over, trying to penetrate vapor, to reach beyond the sounds to whatever it was they designated, the dream guiding the body through the snow, wun-der-lick, object of the inquiry. The air was coarse, leaving a slight burn high in the nostrils. I stepped into a phone booth. Ten yards away a man was urinating against a wall, standing happily in his own cataract and mist.

I spoke to someone downtown, a bored municipal voice, downtown in the huddled buildings, the record sectors, death and taxes, requisition forms, police recruits taping every emergency, bored, bored, the facsimile of a voice, all walls green halfway up, agencies, bureaus, extensions, downtown where the records are kept, massive, passive, ever distending, the *idea* of a voice, no one in control.

I thought of calling Bellevue next but decided finally

in favor of St. Vincent's, gentle, humane and dedicated, St. Vincent's, merciful and compassionate. I insisted on speaking to a nun. I wanted someone who believed in St. Vincent himself, in his ideals, in his sacrifices, whatever these may have been. They wanted address, phone number, sex of deceased. I insisted on a nun. I wanted a nun, a short round woman, perhaps of German descent, someone who believed in the sacredness of dying and the veneration of the dead. No nun, no deal. This is what I told them.

The man was standing outside the phone booth. He wore the plaid lining of someone's topcoat. In his hands was a half-pint bottle of rye, which he offered me. I put down the phone and took it. The snow fell perfectly. Burn marks were evident under the man's frozen stubble. I drank, thanked him and gave back the bottle. Then I called Clobko, who said he'd take care of everything.

Superslick
Mind Contracting
Media Kit

"The Bucky Wunderlick Story"

*Told in news items, lyrics
and dysfunctional interviews*

Prepared by Esme Taylor Associates

A DIVISION OF TRANSPARANOIA

LONDON, April 17 (UPI) — Bucky Wunderlick, the American rock music star, has been held for questioning by police here after allegedly setting fire to a stewardess aboard a TWA 747 just being cleared for takeoff at London Airport.

According to several eyewitnesses, Wunderlick, 24, had complained of being airsick, although the plane had not yet left the ground, and was purportedly acting in a loud and disruptive manner. When Patti Stepney, 22, of Falls Church, Va., one of twelve cabin attendants aboard the London to New York flight, attempted to calm the controversial entertainer, he reputedly set fire to her uniform with a cigarette lighter said by an associate to be a gift of an unidentified member of the British royal family.

The flight was delayed while passengers used blankets to smother the flames, allowing Miss Stepney to be escorted from the 355-ton jetliner by airport personnel. A TWA spokesman later said she was being rushed to a medical facility for observation and possible treatment. Simultaneously, London police released a statement saying they are holding Mr. Wunderlick, who was removed from the plane following a brief struggle, eyewitnesses said.

"Peace-loving men everywhere deplore the English penchant for violence," the internationally known figure was quoted by a companion as having remarked, following another brief altercation inside a police vehicle moments after he was led from the 22-million-dollar jetliner, reportedly bleeding from a gash over his left eye and said to be wearing a team jersey bearing the legend Tottenham Hotspur.

Two tracks from

AMERIKAN WAR SUTRA

Recorded on Beeswax Records
LP 7178342

Bzzz — exclusive trademark of Beeswax Records
Patent pending

VC Sweetheart

Born in a hearse
Left foot first
Nursed on a hand-me-down nipple

Got a murder degree
From I.T.T.
Shot three holes in a cripple

To the highlands I was sent
To the highlands
Flute music playing
They're counting up the dead
Flute music playing in the highlands

Who's that out there
Edging toward the banquet of my dumb fear
Slant eyes burning in this bible bush

VC honey
With her curls and tap shoes
VC sweetheart twirling her baton

She had superdog hearing
And eyes that scanned
I loved every way she made love

Twelve years old
Tiger soul
She knew what to do with a man

Across the highlands we did go
Across the highlands
Blues music playing
They're counting up the dead
Blues music playing in the highlands

She wore black pajamas
And a blade at her hip
So soft and cool and sweet

Twelve years old
Tiger soul
She knew how to cheat and repeat

I sang to her in my own true voice
A folk song of flowers and peace:

What do we have to live for
But each other
What do we have to die for
But our love

East the vanished mountains
West the barren fields

Soccer-playing bodhisattvas
Flowing through the grass

She sang to me in her own true voice
A folk song of people and land:

You are tall lean stranger
You are word
You are Christmas tree of Easter
Shining bird

You are hunter prophet
You are lion's paw
You are angel avenger
Come to my door

Tricky little glitter
In her eyes that night
I made love like a fur-bearing beast

Twelve years old
Tiger soul
She knew how to give what was least

In the highlands we did rest
In the highlands
Jazz music playing
They're counting up the dead
Jazz music playing in the highlands

Sleeping long and deep
On a hard straw mat
I dreamed of the love of my life

Twelve years old
Tiger soul
She knew what to do with a knife

Who's that out there
Edging toward the banquet of my dumb fear
Slant eyes burning in this bible bush

VC honey
With her curls and tap shoes
VC sweetheart twirling her baton

Down the highlands I was sent
Down the highlands
Rock music playing
They're counting up the dead
Rock music playing in the highlands

Born in a hearse
Left foot first
Nursed on a hand-me-down nipple

Got back home
Minus some chrome
Women they call me a cripple

Nothing Turns

Our senses cannot hold them
Nothing turns from death so much as flesh
Oh nothing turns

Nothing turns from death so much as flesh
Untouched by aging

To be younger
Than the children you kill

Sits the ten-star general
There he sits
Ex-vaudevillian
Honing his patter in a cancer ward

Sits the cheesefeet duchess
There she sits
Wombless lady
Cutting paper dolls of burning babes

Nothing turns from death so much as flesh
Untouched by aging

Nothing turns

To be younger than the ones you kill
And remain a velvet child
Too late their cells run wild
General and his lady

You have lost the war
Oh what a bore

You have lost the war
You have lost the war

■

Excerpts from seminar conducted jointly by the senior editorial board of Chance Mainway Publications and the Issues Committee of the Permanent Symposium for the Restoration of Democratic Options.

The Committee	*CM Publications*
Robert Fielder	Sam L. Bradley
Turner Bakey	Ross Holroyd
Grace Hall	Aline Olmstead
Lester E. B. Niles	George Porter
Walter Jencks Olmstead	
Clarence B. Washington	

Special Guest
Bucky Wunderlick

Mr. Fielder: Turning now to our guest at this morning's round table, I'd like to begin by taking this opportunity to welcome him, if I may, to our Chula Vista complex.

BW: Yes, you may.

Mr. Fielder: We're not accustomed so much to this kind of discussion as we are to a different level or range, for example on the freedoms, or House and Senate priorities, or the emerging issue of pleadings and writs. But no phenomenon in recent years in perhaps the whole history of what we might call popular American culture has so brought about a massing of opinion one way or the other among the men and women, and I count myself among them, as do, I'm sure, most if not all the individuals at this morning's round table, about whether or not we can profitably undertake a dialogue with the kind of young people who are at the very center of all this noise, and I hope nobody objects to that word. Please feel free to address yourself to this question in your own words because we're not, although it may seem so to you, the kind of not-with-it people, not at all, the stuffed shirts we may seem so to you, and we've heard this kind of subfamily vernacular, and even the gracious ladies present at this morning's session, I might venture to guess.

BW: Noise, right. It's the sound. Hertz and megahertz. We mash their skulls with a whole lot of watts. Electricity, right. It's a natural force. We're processing a natural force. Electricity is nature every bit as much as sex is nature. By sex, I mean fucking and the like. Electric current is everywhere. We run it through a system of wires, cables, mikes, amps and so on. It's just nature. Sometimes we put words to it. Nobody can hear the words because they get drowned out by the noise, which is only natural. Our last album we recorded live to get the people's screams in and submerge the words even more and they were gibberish words anyway. Screaming's essential to our sound now. The whole thing is nature processed through instruments and sound controls. We process nature, which I personally regard as a hideous screeching bitch of a thing, being a city boy myself.

Miss Hall: Yes, noise. Extraordinary. How, precisely, one wonders, do you do with it what you do with it? I freely confess to a kind of global migraine every time I go anywhere near one of your records. I mean totally apart from the question of decibels, there's that intermixture of instruments or something that's so sort of shattering to one's composure, to put it mildly.

BW: That's why we're so great. We make noise. We make it louder than anybody else and also better. Any curly-haired boy can write windswept ballads. You have to crush people's heads. That's the only way to make those fuckers listen.

Mr. Porter: But what I'm really trying to get at, really, I think, is the more basic question of human values, human concerns.

Mr. Holroyd: I think what George is really trying to get at is the effect of this type of thing . . .

Mr. Porter: No, no, no, no, no.

Mr. Bakey: Lunch.

Mrs. Olmstead: Do you consider yourself an artist?

BW: The true artist makes people move. When people read a book or look at a painting, they just sit there or stand there. A long time ago that was okay, that was hip, that was art. Now it's different. I make people move. My sound lifts them right off their ass. I make it happen. Understand. I make it happen. What I'd like to do really is I'd like to injure people with my sound. Maybe actually kill some of them. They'd come there knowing full well. Then we'd play and sing and people in the audience would be frozen with pain or writhing with pain and some of them would actually die from the effects of our words and music. It isn't an easy thing to create, the right sound at the proper volume. People actually collapsing in pain. They'd come there knowing full well. People dying from the effects of all this beauty and power. That's art, sweetheart. I make it happen.

Mr. Niles: At this point I suspect you're only being half-serious.

BW: Which half?

Mr. Bakey: You're not saying, or are you, that the only thing you do is make loud noises and this is what explains the Wunderlick formulation or ethos.

BW: My whole life is tinged with melancholy. The more I make people move, the closer I get to personal inertness. With everybody jumping the way they do and holding their heads in the manner they're inclined to hold their heads, I feel in kind of a mood of melancholy because I myself am kind of tired of all the movement and would like to flatten myself against a wall and become inert.

Miss Hall: Quite so.

Mr. Bradley: I wonder if you'd like to discuss the origin and meaning of the phrase pee-pee-maw-maw. I know it's traceable to you and it seems to be sweeping the country at the moment. Everywhere I go, and I do extensive traveling, I see people wearing shirts and trousers with those little syllables on them, not to mention seeing pee-pee-maw-maw on shopping bags, buttons, decals, bumper stickers, and even hearing dolls say it over and over, five-dollar talking dolls that say that phrase over and over. I know it's all traceable to you and I just wonder what it all signifies, if anything.

BW: Childhood incantation.

Mr. Bakey: Ah.

Mrs. Olmstead: Perhaps you'd care to elaborate.

BW: As a little kid in the street I used to hear older kids saying it. It's one of the earliest memories of my life. Older kids playing in the street at night. I'd be on the stoop or watching from a window. Too little to play with the older kids. Summer nights on the street in New York. Very early memory. These kids chanting to each other. Pee-pee-maw-maw. I don't think anybody knew what it meant or where it came from. Probably twelfth century England or the Vikings or the Moors. These kids chanting it on the street. Pee-pee-maw-maw. Pee-pee-maw-maw. Chants like that can be traced to the dawn of civilization. Like games kids play can be traced a thousand years back to kids in India. Same with incantations. It's an interesting subject. You should schedule it.

Mr. Fielder: For my closing remarks, which I promise you will be kept as brief as humanly possible, given the pronounced oratorical bias of your speaker and chairman, I'd like simply to say that this has been a most dynamic round table, surely for me a most instructive one as well, as it was I believe for all of us gathered here, although each no doubt has his or her own idea of levels of merit, remembering our own Turner Bakey and his oft-quoted rejoinder to Eddings' paraphrase of Larue during the Arts-Leadership Committee's brunch on genocide. At any rate, thanks one and all. And now for a dip in the pool.

■

Three tracks from

DIAMOND STYLUS

Recorded on Anspar Records & Tapes
International copyright secured

Cold War Lover

I worked her body with a touch
Learned from the hand of a blind old man
Living in a one-room duplex
In Nashville's Chinatown

It was love truest love
Under gun
One by one
She was the butch of New Orleans
I was her sometime beau

In those murderbeds of pimps and tricks
All those ranting nights
We took what was and left the rest
And mailed the short hairs east to west

Oh funky city
Funky city oh

We loved each other with a heat
Learned from the tongue of a strung-out tout
Squatting in a two-room toilet
In Tulsa's Upper Crust

It was love animal love
Under lock
Rock by rock
She was the butch of New Orleans
I was her sometime beau

In those murderbeds of queens and marks
Sultry afternoons
We said a prayer and took a hit
And went to church to nod a bit

Oh funky city
Funky city oh

She washed my body with a grace
Learned from the rub of a burnt-out case
Locked in a padded tub
In the Memphis Steamless Baths

It was love animal love
Under key
Three by three
She was the butch of New Orleans
I was her sometime beau

In those murderbeds of cons and pros
All those summer days
We reached the end and bent the wick
And placed an ad for stamps to lick

Oh funky city
Funky city oh

We broke each other with a skill
Learned from the mind of a kindly dike
Stuck in an airless shaft
In Harlem's Lonely Heart

It was love truest love
Cannibal war
More and more
She was the butch of New Orleans
I was her sometime beau

In those murderbeds of men and wives
Final quickest trip

She took a gun, a thirty-one
Put her tongue to the bluesteel tip

Oh funky cities
Mobile's paper mills
I swim in the bay
And get laid by day
And cry for my love all the night

Protestant Work Ethic Blues

Rising up in the morning
Looking down at yourself in bed
Oh rising up in the morning
Seeing your pale old body matter-of-factually dead
Oh blue
Never too white to sing the blues

Getting yourself together
Pulling day and night apart
Oh getting yourself together
Staring hard at your laminated astrological chart
Oh blue
Never too white to sing the blues

Sitting up in your plastic chair
Swallowing down some frozen toast
Oh catching that old broken window train
Take you to the place
The place
The place
Take you to the place that you hate the most

Oh yeah

Protestant work ethic blues
You got those white collar blues

Dropping down behind your desk
Crumpled in a puddly heap
Oh dropping down behind your desk
Waiting for the strength to take that existential leap
Oh blue
Never too white to sing the blues

Falling off to sleep and weep
In your three-poster bed
Oh falling off to deep dark sleep
You find yourself wearing a mask over your original
    head
Oh blue
Never too white to sing the blues

Protestant work ethic blues
Tough to shake those blues

Diamond Stylus

Sounds I see
Breaking through the hard light
Razor notes
Close to someone's throat
Re-ject
Is the mark along the arm
Long-play
Is the enemy

Songs I touch
Wheeling through the soft night
Tracking force
Is the way I die

It scratched out lines on my face
Test pressing time
It pained me so it pained me so
Drying out the vinyl

Sound is hard to child-bear
Skin inked black
Turning into burning thing
Circling into wordtime

Words I taste
Dripping through the knife's bite
Needle tracks
Marking up the snow
Re-volve
Is the time I have to live
Ma-trix
Is the mother-cut

Notes I play
Twinkling through the bird's flight
Tracking force
Is the way I die

They give me five hundred hours
One thousand sides
Numbering down the broken sounds
Scratching out a life

Sound is hard to child-bear
Skin inked black
Turning into burning thing
Circling into wordtime

Sounds I see
Breaking through the hard light
Razor notes
Close to someone's throat
Re-ject
Is the mark along the arm
Long-play
Is the enemy

Complete transcript of interview conducted by Steven Grey, editor-in-chief of Ibex, *a Journal of Rock Art.*

GREY: Hey, man, glad you could make it over. Just like to start off the proceedings by asking a couple or three questions about the mountain tapes. Are you figuring to just sit on this material or is there a release date for this material or what? It's been a long time between releases and people are starting to wonder about that and in a business like our business you hear all kinds of things and I wanted to start off by asking straight out . . .

WUNDERLICK: (*garbled*)

GREY: Could you try to aim your words right at the thing there? Where you going? Hey, man, where you going?

WUNDERLICK: (*garbled*)

GREY: Hey, man. Aw, hey. Aw, come on back, man. Aw, no. Aw, hey. We just got . . . we just . . . aw, man, no.

ROCK STAR REVEALS SWEATER FETISH!!!
by Carmela Bevilacqua

After I'd interviewed hard-to-interview Bucky Wunderlick in his spectacular mountain retreat overlooking a shimmering lake in the rugged, scenic Adirondacks, I came away feeling just a mite dazed by his gentleness and quiet charm. After all, the supercharged world of rock 'n' roll isn't my usual beat, in addition to which everybody knows how difficult and temperamental Bucky is supposed to be, so imagine how delightfully surprised I was by his feather-soft nature. In fact it was a day full of surprises, including a strange and bizarre visit from an unexpected guest.

But to get back to the beginning, maybe "interview" is the wrong word. Bucky didn't actually answer any of my questions. Formal answers, no. But talk to me he certainly did! Nodding his head slowly at my queries about his personal and professional life, Bucky chatted slowly and with a kind of sleepy charm about his dreams and his fears, about music and love and poetry, about people, oceans, streets and trees. Such was the hypnotic quality of his voice that at times it was difficult to catch what he was saying. Sometimes his voice would drop

115

away to a whisper and other times he just seemed to ramble on, stringing words together in an aimless pattern. As Bucky talked, his lady of the hour drifted in and out, occasionally joining the conversation. Since you're probably dying to know, I won't waste any time telling you that she's slim and dusty-blond, and she goes by the name of Mazola June. ("They named me after the corn oil," she said in a lil ole drawl of a voice.) After she drifted off thataway, I asked Bucky to fill in the details on this female friend of marriageable age.

"We're running death sprints," he said mysteriously, and although I tried to prod him on the subject of marriage in the near future and the possibility of children and a life far removed from the tawdry glitter, he never returned to the subject of his pretty (and private) companion.

It was about this time that one of Bucky's ever-present aides, flunkies or what-have-you came slouching in to report that "some creep" had breached security and was hanging around in the hall outside, hoping to be granted an audience with the star himself. Bucky replied with a shrug and the intruder was ushered in. He was a smallish, pale man and he looked directly into Bucky's eyes, spoke four sentences and then left without waiting for a reply.

"What you have to teach is greater than our capacity to learn. You must stop so we can understand what you've been doing. I've come a thousand miles to see you. Now begins the long wait until you come to me."

Later, Bucky and I watched the sun sink into the

lake in a riotous blaze of color. I asked him about his obviously undeserved reputation for controversy and mayhem, and when he made no reply other than a clown's sad smile, I wondered aloud how difficult it must be for him to occupy the stormy heights of his profession, how hard to endure the constant stress of being number one in a business where the roadside is strewn with casualties.

"Wear sweaters," Bucky said softly in the fading glow of twilight, sitting just a yard away from me on the spacious patio behind the house in the gathering chill. "Sweaters absorb the major impact. I wear three and sometimes four sweaters everywhere I go, weather permitting. Not on stage. I'm not talking about on stage. On stage you've got to be naked at the moment of impact. That's the moment of ultimate truth and ultimate falsehood, and the only way to go is go naked. Off stage, I wear sweaters. One on top of the other. All kinds. Three and four and sometimes five sweaters."

Mazola June came out then, wrapped in the longest scarf I've ever seen in my life, and before too long they'd both nodded off to dreamy sleep, right there in front of me, a pair of babes in the northern wood.

Title track from

PEE-PEE-MAW-MAW

Recorded on Anspar Records & Tapes
International copyright secured

Pee-Pee-Maw-Maw

Blank mumble blat
Babble song babble song
Foaming at the mouth
Won ton soupie

Spit gargle retch
Easter bunny juke puke
Family zoo me and you
Moo moo moo

The beast is loose
Least is best
Pee-pee-maw-maw

The beast is loose
Least is best
Pee-pee-maw-maw

Nil nully void
Biting down on hankychiffs
Where's the end round this bend
Scream dream baby

Boo holler hoot
Picking on the ear string
Cut a slice of steel guitar
Spang bang clang

The beast is loose
Least is best
Pee-pee-maw-maw

The beast is loose
Least is best
Pee-pee-maw-maw
Pee-pee-maw-maw

12

WHEN I LIVED in the mountains I had a special room built into the studio portion of my house. It was an anechoic chamber, absolutely soundproof and free of vibrations. The whole room was bedded on springs and lined with fiberglass baffles that absorbed all echo. There I listened to tapes of my own material, both in transition stage and final form. Music was a liquid presence in that chamber, invisible wine for the ear to taste. I used the room often but not always to play the tapes. Sometimes I just sat there, wedged in a block of silence, trying to avoid the feeling that time is stretchable. The small room seemed a glacial waste, bounded only by solid materials, subject to no central thesis, far more frighteningly immaculate than it was when pure music skated from the tapes. If you could stretch a given minute, what would you find between its unstuck components? Probably some kind of astral madness. A bleak comprehension of the final size of things. The room yielded no real secrets, of course, and provided no more than a hint of the nature of silence itself. There was always something to hear, even in that shaved air, the earth roiling into a turn, cells in my body answering to war.

Azarian came from Los Angeles to offer condolences. He climbed the stairs, shook hands with me, stood at the far end of the room. Somewhere along the way he had been given official word; her death was natural, coming as a result of unrelenting neglect. An acute pancreatic infection, viral pneumonia, an intestinal obstruction, a noninfectious kidney disease centered in the blood vessels of that organ. I wondered how much pain she'd endured in order to comply with her own cruel rudiments of conduct. Attrition. Let the stress of trying to live determine how you die. Ride along and hope it doesn't hurt too much. The intransigence of an enchanted child. Loving the child, I'd been half in fear of the woman, knowing she was serious, an unbroken line defining whatever it was she'd hoped to gain or lose. Someone to measure myself against. Azarian went on to say that Globke had contacted the family and arranged for the body to be sent back home, air freight express.

"What are you doing in L.A.?" I said.

"Tremendous things. I probably shouldn't tell you about it. In fact I'm determined not to."

"What is it?"

"Blackness."

"Black music?"

"Black everything," Azarian said. "Blackness as such."

"What's it like being into blackness."

"I'm not too far into it yet. But I'm making my way, little by little. I really shouldn't be talking about it. It's really deep, Bucky. Deep and dark. It's pressing against me with tremendous weight, practically crushing my chest. A lot of fear is involved. All kinds of fear. It's hard to pick out a single moment when I'm not afraid."

"How do you get into something like blackness? Do you have to shed your whiteness first? Or do you just go hurtling forward, bang, and risk all kinds of injury, mind and body?"

"How do I get into blackness? Is that what you're asking?"

"Can you put it in words?" I said.

"It's a street thing. Blackness is a street thing. It's the self-identification of the people on the street. Watts is a whole big bunch of streets. Same with Bed-Stuy. Harlem, it's not so much the streetness of Harlem, it's more the history and the badness of the vibes. Black is baddest in the best sense. I mean that's where you have to go to make sense of the magic of existence. You pass through all that streetness and weight and terror and you come out a more dimensional person."

"But how do you get into blackness, being nonblack?"

"I can't put it in words," he said.

I pointed toward a chair but he said he preferred to stand. He seemed to avoid looking directly at me. The curse in the eyes of the bereaved. I watched puddles form under his boots as a series of tiny ice slides occurred.

"How's the band?"

"We're laying down vocals," he said. "Still plenty of contract problems though. I don't know at this point who we're recording for. People come in screaming at us. When are you making it back out?"

"Not yet. I've been set back. Have to reassemble myself."

"Bucky, these people I represent. They're real interested in getting their hands on the product we spoke about last time I was here."

"Talk to Happy Valley."

"I'm afraid to, Bucky. It's not just fear of being physically hurt or maimed for life. It's the whole idea of who they are that scares me."

"Who are they?"

"You know that better than I do. You've been in touch with them. They hired Opel to deal for them. At this late date you know more about them than I do. In other words you're the one that should talk to them. I know you're in mourning or whatever the hip equivalent of mourning is. So obviously you've got other things on your mind and I appreciate the fact that if you don't want to do business right now, there's a time and place. But if I go in there and talk to Happy Valley on my own, anything and everything might and can happen, especially since there's been a split in their own ranks."

"That makes things more interesting," I said. "You can play one side against the other."

"Are you crazy? I wouldn't get involved in anything like that. Are you crazy?"

"Why don't you stick to music then?"

"I am sticking to music, Bucky. Being into blackness the way I am, I'm getting interested in root forms of rock 'n' roll. I'm beginning to delve real deep in that area. But I also have this other part of my life that I'm trying to find a place for. There's so much to be afraid of in contemporary society. I'm establishing a permanent relationship with these people I've mentioned on the Coast in order, among other things, to examine and find the sources of my own fear. Together we've come up with a plan whereby you with your influence and mystique can make an offer to the Happy Valley Farm Commune, this or that faction, flip a coin, whoever's got control of the product, and you can do it without letting on that I'm involved or my people on the Coast are involved or anybody's involved except who you say the involved party is. Do you want to hear the details?"

I shook my head and once again pointed out a chair. Azarian wanted to stand, remaining in a far corner, apparently trying to avoid the center of the room, an area he seemed to regard as dangerous, if not totally unapproachable, Opel's deathly fumes still clinging to furniture and choice belongings, and he talked of the old days, his uncomplicated fame, the girls who walked in and out of his bed, several every night, coming and going like popcorn vendors at a circus. We shook hands again. Then he went uptown to be interviewed on stereo FM.

13

NOTHING CHANGED, altered or varied. There were no plants in the room to climb or die. I saw no insects. Sleet struck the window with sparse fragile impact and all demolition in the area was halted by weather. Time did not seem to pass as much as build, slowly gathering weight. This was the sole growth in the room and against it hung the silence, peeled back to reveal the white nightmares voiced on the floor below. I tried to remember places and things. Rain on the runway of the international airport. Rain on the simulated hamlet. Rain in the terminal province. Rain at vespers in the heliport near the river. Rain in the abstract garden. Rain in the boots of the bitch in Munich. Rain on the nameless moor.

I returned to the radio, to watching the firehouse, to becoming fixed in place. The artist sits still, finally, because the materials he deals with begin to shape his life, instead of being shaped, and in stillness he seeks a form of self-defense, one that ends with putrefaction, or stillness caught in time lapse. But I wasn't quite at that point in my career. I dreamed a return to the old palaces, the great jaded hulks of rock 'n' roll, boarded up but still standing, as far as I knew, in this city and that, always on the edge of comatose slums.

A man came to see me. He was wrapped in a double-breasted suit and high tight shirt collar. His custom-styled hair was rigid and thick, sprayed into place and fitted trimly over his forehead — a work of Renaissance masonry, it seemed. He stood in the doorway, coat over his arm, earnest hand waiting to be taken.

"Who are you?"

"ABC," he said.

"Forget it."

"Nothing big or elaborate. An abbreviated interview. Your televised comments on topics of interest. Won't take ten minutes. We're all set up downstairs. Ten minutes. You've got my word, Bucky. The word of a personal admirer."

"Positively never."

"I've got a slot on the local mid-morning news. In case you didn't catch the face. I do youth events and youth personalities. Sure, it's the same old commercial brainwash that we've all been fighting against but on the other hand the only way we can get exposure for certain voices is to slip them into little scheduling cracks here and there. It's a question of easing the pressure the different slots exert on each other and then slipping in there with the visionaries, the prophets if you will, the authentic non-bullshit voices. Ten minutes of televised question and answer. Frankly I've been researching hell out of you."

"No."

"I haven't done this kind of massive research since I've been in the glamour end of the business. I used to be in the ass end. But there's a softening in the market as old faces crumble and new slots become available. I'm trying to fill some of these slots with youth-oriented conceptuals. Bucky, just your unrehearsed comments on the rumors, the whereabouts, the future plans if any. What I'm making is really a small demand on your time. Frankly it barely qualifies as a demand, considering the demands I'm accustomed to making."

"Maybe later in the decade."

"Your power is growing, Bucky. The more time you spend in isolation, the more demands are made on the various media to communicate some relevant words and pictures. We make demands on you not because we're media leeches of whatever media but frankly because proportionate demands are being made on us. People want words and pictures. They want images. Your power grows. The less you say, the more you are. But this is an obvious truism of the industry and I didn't come down here to present my credentials as some kind of theorist or moneychanger in ideas. I'm an on-camera entity. I do my thing and go to black. It's a complicated way to live. Let me tell you in ten words or less what I've got downstairs."

"Can it wait?"

"I've got camera and I've got sound," he said. "They're down there in the street. Cameraman, soundman, both top people, artists if you will. We'd like to do the interview directly in front of the building. We do a vertical pan down the building right to you and me. We're standing there in the sleet. I'm holding an umbrella over both of us as we talk."

He looked at my hands and then my face, as if checking flesh tones and textures to measure against his camera's passion, the nibbling skills of its enormous jaws.

"Come back when I'm not here," I said. "It'll be easier. You can do whatever you want."

"I'm really anxious to fill those slots, Bucky. Your power grows. I hate to think of all those slots going unfilled. What'll we put in there? We've used clips of rock festivals absolutely everywhere but in the Okefenokee Swamp and I'm sure that's next with everybody either getting typhoid or ripped apart by alligators."

"That's an interesting shirt you're wearing."

"This shirt I'm wearing? This shirt is a knit concept. Higher neckband than the average knit. Treble-button cuffs. Strong coloration. Snug body-fit. It's a Scandinavian import and it totals out at twenty-two ninety-five. Take a look at my face."

"Why?"

"Take a look at my face. Go ahead, a close look. Now what do you see?"

"I don't know," I said.

"You see healthy pores. You see pores that aren't clogged. How do I do it, right? I've got a facial-aid skin machine. This is a device for cleansing pores of all the pollutants in the air. It blasts pollutants right out of the holes in the face. Why do I take the trouble, right? Listen, I'm on camera an average of three minutes total every day of the week six days a week. That tells you everything. The heat. The lights. The tension. The sweat. The tight close-ups. Now it begins to make sense, right? The skin machine. The accessory pore-brush. The clear gel peel-away mask. The deep dissolving nonallergenic soap. I make it my business to communicate a crisp image. Do you want me to tell you how I knew you were here?"

"No."

"Somebody talked," he said. "Somebody's pushing. Somebody's trying to get you out of here. But meanwhile it's time for me to get back uptown. Shame to waste that slot. God bless, despite everything. So long now. See you soon. Peace."

"War," I said.

I listened to the radio. Announcers took turns reciting the same news reports. Each man gave way to the next man in the series until a cycle was completed. Wording was altered only slightly and vocal tones remained consistent all through the hour. Out of a nest of static came a new voice now, fantastic and savage, beautiful to my ear, churning with gastric power.

"*Lissen what I say, bay-bee, this be Doo-Wop here, bop and groove, yow yow yow, lissen what I say but no do what I do, boogie with your footie, ay chihuahua, stone gold monster music, down and round, popping at my console, Doo-Wop bay-bee, lissen and live, stone gold number eight, Bad Jasper Brown with Mama Mama Mama, jive and dive, Doo-Wop bopping your dead head, yow yow yow, stone gold eight, mama mama what's it all mean, Bad Jasper, cut me down.*"

Hanes visited then. His exemplary fatigue made him appear even younger than he was, stylish boy of the boulevards, intelligent and frail, ever ready to renounce even his own spectral pleasures, a voluptuary indulging himself in the idea of restraint. He was carrying a Macy's shopping bag.

"Regrets et cetera," he said. "She was just beginning to

accept me as a person. She even said she might eventually learn to like me. I have no reason to believe it wouldn't have worked out — Opel and I working together."

"Did you come for the package?"

"There's a corpo on the steps outside."

"Must be recent," I said.

"His head's been bashed."

"We need Florence Nightingale to come back and tell us how to deal with these matters."

"I may get an eight-track stereo cartridge recorder. What kind do you recommend I get? It's the one thing my music system's missing. Don't let money interfere with your line of thought. I may very soon be in a position to afford pretty much the best."

"I'm not up on things," I said.

"You're missing a lot. There's a lot going on. It's all under the surface, of course. Surface events are practically nil. But that doesn't mean nothing's going on. Incidentally you were seen in three different cities in England day before yesterday. And you're buried in an unmarked grave in rural Montana. As opposed to urban Montana, I guess."

"The rumors are getting a little sloppy."

"Poetic is the word according to Globke. But things keep going. Things haven't let up at all. The press is still having the dry heaves over your disappearance. The underground press. The radical press. The trade press. The straight press. The revolutionary press."

"It can't be much of a disappearance. ABC was here this morning. Do you want the package or not?"

"Do I want the package or not? Well now that's not the easiest question to answer. I do want the package, yes. But what do I want to do with it? Now that's something else. I've been given a plane ticket and certain instructions. But there are other courses I might pursue. These people known as Happy Valley aren't necessarily prepared to understand every little nuance of the situation. I mean presumably the thing is up for bidding. It's a free market, isn't it? There are subtleties. Maybe somebody is prepared to bid on this product. There are nuances. There are ambiguities. Life itself is sheer ambiguity. If a person doesn't see that, he's either an asshole or a fascist."

"But you'll take the package with you."

"Absolutely," he said. "I'll do that absolutely. In fact I leave on vacation in a matter of hours. Point or points unknown. Globke will have to get along without me for the next few weeks. Actually I haven't made my big decision yet. I want to wait till the last minute. This flight or that. I may choose to take my seat at the negotiating table with Dr. Pepper. Or I may decide to deal on my own. Straight salary gets to be boring, tax structures being what they are. So who knows? I may risk all."

"Florence Nightingale and a whole lot of bandages."

He raised the shopping bag.

"Here, take this," he said.

"What is it?"

"It's the product."

The package he took from the shopping bag looked the same as the one in the trunk. Brown wrapping paper. Brown gummed tape. Same size. Roughly the same weight. Hanes displayed his amusement by putting his hand to his face and gazing into the middle distance.

"Opel," I said.

"Very good. Excellent. I didn't think you'd know. She gave it to me when I was last here. You were sleeping the sleep of the innocent. She told me to call it the product. I don't normally approve of private jokes. But in this case, two people I've admired — why not? Apparently she was going to leave it here for you to find once we were on our way to Pepperland. She had no intention of coming back here, as you may or may not know. When we finished with Dr. Pepper she planned to head directly for Spain. Eventually you'd find the package and that would be the end of the little joke. But when the courier turned out to be an old acquaintance, namely myself, she thought it would be a nice idea to embellish the joke by having me deliver the goods. I have no idea what's in there and don't intend to ask. To be opened when the Glob begins to menace. Her words. When the Glob begins to menace."

"Whatever it is, it's my birthday present."

"Happy birthday," he said. "But I want you to know I'm disappointed you don't have any advice for me on what kind of cartridge recorder to get. I love to get advice from people at the top of a particular professional heap. Any kind of advice from such people I find is worth listening to."

"Any kind at all?"

"Absolutely," he said.

"Be willing to die for your beliefs, or computer printouts of your beliefs."

"That's nearly a very interesting remark," Hanes said.

I opened the trunk, gave him the original package and replaced it with Opel's gift. That night there was a woman in the hall when I went down the stairs. She was in the process of opening the door to the first floor apartment. Her galoshes, with shoes inside them, were set against the wall, dripping snow, and she stood in bare feet and sorted through the keys in her handbag. She was a short compact woman whose ankles seemed to have a special density. I nodded to her — the kind of greeting exchanged by men confined in submarines for long periods.

"I'm the woman downstairs," she said. "Up-on-three told me there was a new person. You're not noisy, that's for sure. If it's too cold, hit the pipes. Micklewhite. Downstairs from you."

"Right."

"I been here it seems like a hundred years. My husband used to be the super. But he died of complications. I take care of sending up the heat. If you get cold, hit twice on the pipes. My kid inside isn't normal. Don't worry if you hear noises."

"It doesn't get very loud."

"My husband had all kinds of cockamamie ideas. First off he wanted to sell the kid to a carnival. But who'd buy him? They wouldn't be able to sell enough tickets for all the trouble it takes to take care of him. Then he wanted to rent him out to colleges where they have doctors and nurses studying in there. I put the kibosh on that. I said you're dreaming. I said nobody wants to look at this kid. I said the only thing to do is leave him here and keep the door closed."

"What's his name?" I said.

"His name? He don't have a name. We never figured he'd live past four months with a head like his head. But did we get fooled. Did we get stuck with a lemon. My husband, he figured make the best of it. Find an

134

interested party and either sell the kid outright or lease him by the month. Carnivals, they have seasons. Take him, bring him back, take him, bring him back. You should have seen that s.o.b. He used to work out schemes and plans and arrangements, left and right. I said hooey. I said you're dreaming. I said you'll have to go to the booby hatch to find an interested party. He wanted to take out ads, my husband. Carnivals, they have special newspapers. He kept working out plans and more plans and more plans until the day he keeled over. You should have seen him keel over. It was just after the second operation. Tessie was here, the candy store's daughter. We watched him keel right over. I told Tessie I said I bet it's complications. But he had big plans. You should have seen him talk. He was only this big but he had a mouth on him like a power saw. I'll tell you what he was because you wouldn't guess it if you saw him. He was a horse pervert. He went to the track rain or shine. Him and the chink from the Bronx, they went to the track in blizzards with their hats down over their ears. He lost thirty, forty simoleons on the average every time they went. The chink had winners left and right. The chink knew the scratch sheet, he knew the smart money, he knew the track, he knew the weather, he knew the animals. My husband, he didn't know shit from Shinola. He'd starve himself half to death to save enough money to give it to a horse. But don't mind my mouth. I talk and talk and never know what's coming out. It's loneliness, that's all it is. It's living with someone that can't form a word."

I tried to remember what I was doing on the stairs. I had my lumber jacket on but I didn't know where I was headed. I stayed outside the building for a while. A man in a long coat stood in the alley between Lafayette and Broadway. When I went back upstairs it was quiet everywhere. No bowel sounds in the plumbing and little of Fenig tracing his way to productivity. The man from ABC had left his card on the table. Although I'd never seen him on television I was able to recall almost every detail of his appearance. He possessed that high gloss common to interchangeable celebrities, to the male secretaries of important female executives, to lawyers with connections in show business. His clothes had seemed extremely tight, equipped with hidden straps, and he hadn't changed expression for the course of his visit. Television. Maybe it was all a study in the art of mummification. The effect of the medium is so evanescent that those who work in its time apparatus feel the need to preserve themselves, delivering their bodies to be lacquered and trussed, sprayed with the rarest of pressurized jellies, all to one end, a release from the perilous context of time. This is their only vanity, to expect to dwell forever in hermetic subcorridors, free of every ravage, secure as old kings asleep in sodium.

I undressed for the first time in two days, getting into bed naked and weak, unfamiliar with my own body. Fenig began then, taking long and desperate strides, and the soft boy below, Micklewhite's carnival meat, cried four times in the making of a dream.

14

HASHISH smoked in motels always seemed mean. I remember the feeling of something in the middle of my head trying to expand, to work itself outward, causing fearsome pressure. We were in motels between flights or performances, or between a flight and a performance, or the other way around. The motel was never quite the same but motel time was identical everywhere we stayed. There were no edges to the tensions of our waiting; it was one blank plane of unsegmented time. We were usually located somewhere on the outskirts of a vast population center (not necessarily a city) and we sat on the bed or floor, never in chairs, sucking up bad hash, waiting for the ever-rumored limousine to come slipping in out of the plastic glades, a comically elegant hearse into which seven or eight bodies might eventually drop, musicians, road managers, long blond girls with perfect legs, most of us in soiled old clothes, mendicant's denim and mauled boots, all rank with weed, trying to encompass the range of inconsistencies and finding this an unworthwhile endeavor.

But it's the rooms we waited in that I recall. Their plainness had a center to it, a remote secret, something one might seek to reach only through the unbent energies of certain drugs. It was a strange thing about hashish used in this environment; it seemed a puppet drug of technology, made and marketed under government supervision, a contingency weapon devised by some hobbyist of the nastier industrial echelons. Nothing was safe and there was no sure way to the center. I became both frightened and totally immobile, distrustful of everyone in the room, growing heavier by the second. A grim organic motor pulsed against the walls of my head. Often I tried to reason my way out of this conjuncture of fear and stone-weight. But there were too many areas of concentrated pressure, there was too much *gravity* in the universe, and although I never reconciled myself to whatever horror was ultimate I could not resist the systematic truth that I was being subsumed into an even more immobile category, that of chair, bed, room or motel itself. (It was after one of these half-hours of pensive insanity that I came up with the name Transparanoia for our spreading inkblot of holding companies, trusts, acquisitions and cabals.) In the plainest of rooms nothing was comprehensible. We waited to be taken to a sports arena, convention center, theater or stadium, there to plug ourselves in, to run the lucky hum through our blood, to give them evil meat to eat, the blind maidens naked on Styrofoam pedestals, the sellers of ancient medicines, the masters of trance, the black stoics exhibiting their puncture marks, the knifemen and poisoners, every head melting in the warp of our sound, its deflected electric howl, ladies screaming from wheelchairs, children in drag, feeble-minded bankers, wine merchants and baby rapers, mystics in heat, translucent boys fondling the tits of missionaries' wives. They pressed against each other, chained to their invisible history, the youngest among them knowing of all needs that one is uppermost, the need to be illiterate in the land of the self-erasing word.

For the first time in weeks Fenig was sitting at the top of the landing. I paused at my door, feeling certain there was something he wanted to say.

"Every pornographic work brings us closer to fascism."

I went inside, not bothering to lock the door. In a little while he came in. It was a dark afternoon and I lit a candle. Fenig sat at the edge of a straight-backed chair, leaning well forward, easily able to put his fingers to the tips of his tennis sneakers.

"Many thanks," he said.

"What for?"

"For listening."

"I had to stop anyway to get the door opened. So it wasn't that much of an ordeal. Haven't seen you, Eddie. Pounding away at the old machine. Is that what you've been doing?"

"You called me Eddie. That's a gracious gesture and I appreciate it. Coming from you, Bucky, tops in your trade, it's not the kind of thing I'm ever likely to forget. Is there some coffee you can give me?"

"I haven't been able to find the coffee."

"I'd be happy to consume the dregs from an old cup that's just lying around unwashed."

"Sorry."

"I'm in the middle of a dark period, practically black. It's one of those times in a writer's life when he or she just wants to fall into bed and pull the covers over his or her head. I'm dropping all my genres and going into a new one completely. The kiddie filth didn't pan out. I can't sell a thing. I can't make anything happen. It's all going sour and I'm just beginning to suspect the reason. Maybe I'll have more on that next time we get together. But for now suffice it to say I'm in deep trouble."

"How deep?"

"How deep is deep, Bucky? The very depths. The place where no sunlight reaches. The pressure hole of the great ocean trench. I'm surrounded by blind fish swimming all around me. It's colder than mountains."

"The pacing hasn't helped. Is that right?"

"There was a point there and I shouldn't admit this even to you, Bucky, but there was a point there when I actually did some running and jumping. I told myself it was exercise, exercise. But I knew deep down it was an extreme form of pacing, an attempt to reinvigorate the format. Now I'm back to conventional pacing again so maybe all is not total blackness just yet. I've written in many styles and in great quantity. I used to turn out material by the yard and they used to pay me by the yard. I don't know what's happened. I know I haven't priced myself out of the market. I know I haven't lost my willingness to work. But the fact remains I can't sell a thing lately. Rejections every which way. It must be an inner failing. Pornography caused the original trouble. That much I know. I got lost in P-ville and I couldn't get out with my professionalism intact. I'm just now beginning to understand the factors and motivations behind my lack of inspiration, for lack of a better word, but that's another story for another season. If there's anything I am, it's professional. Take that away and I turn into an amorphous mass of undifferentiated matter. There's a cruel kind of poetry to the market. The big wheel spins and gyrates and makes fire-cracker noises, going faster and faster and throwing off anybody who can't hold on. The market is rejecting me but I'm not blind to the cruel poetry in it. The market is phenomenal, bright as a hundred cities, turning and turn-ing, and there are little figures everywhere trying to hold on with one hand but they're getting thrown off into the surrounding night, the silence, the emptiness, the darkness, the basin, the crater, the pit. But the son of a bitch won't get rid of me that easy. I'm a tenacious brute for my size. I'm an in-fighter who can hold his own, pound for pound. I know the ups and downs of this business like few men in my time. But I appreciate your calling me Eddie. This is a big thing to an emotional person like me, which is basically what I am, and I want you to know I'll remem-ber. Everybody else forgets but I remember."

"I can't offer advice for your comeback."

"I'll tell you what you can do," he said. "You can find the coffee pot you used last time you made coffee and maybe there's some grounds left over in the ground holder and you can give me a paper napkin and I can saturate the napkin with soggy coffee grounds and just hold it un-der my nose and sniff it for a little while."

"Aside from everything else I don't think I have any napkins."

"The paper kind is what I need."

"Even if there are some, I haven't seen any coffee grounds lately."

"Fame, riches, greatness, immortality."

We sat through a long period of silence. Fenig tugged on the laces used to tighten the hood of his sweatshirt. He took his own pulse, right thumb on left wrist. He ran his tongue over the hair on the back of his hand. Then he made an odd sound. *Warp.* I leaned toward him.

"What's wrong?"

"Sick to my stomach," he said. "It's a characteristic of every dark period I go through. This is the absolute middle of it. The cold ocean trench. Not being able to start something new. Warp. It's happened before but never this bad. Genetically blind fish."

"Some water maybe."

"I'll be all right in a minute."

"You don't look good."

"Warp."

"Something to drink, Eddie."

"I'd better get upstairs. I thought it was sinking back into my stomach but maybe it's not. Upstairs would be best. Warp. I don't like to inflict my creative tensions on other people. Best if I went upstairs."

"Yes," I said.

The bed was a vast welcoming organism, a sea culture or synthetic plant, enraptured by the object it absorbed. As I headed deeper into mists and old stories, into windy images poised on the rim of sleep, I began to feel that the bed was having a dream and that the dream was me. One candle burned, this light not quite eluding my awareness. I was barely conscious, being dreamed by a preternatural entity, taken for a mind's ride into the mystery of things. It was all a question of control. I was being dreamed-smoked-created. The dream took form as a man asleep in a bed situated in the middle of a room in which a lone candle burned. This was not real but a dream and I was no more than the stale chemical breath of the dreamer.

The essential question was one of control. I went deeper now, struggling to produce a dream of my own, to return from those dim midlands with the fire of legend and sex contained in a thimble, safe for men to use. I was suspended in a double moment, trying to free myself, when suddenly a fierce noise broke over the bed, a wild ringing that lifted me through levels of consciousness out into the cold open room. Telephone. It seemed incredible and I merely stared at the sucking black shape. Each note seemed louder and more shrill, the protest cry of a thing that preferred its latent state. Telephone. I walked across the floor and picked up the receiver.

"What do you want? Who is this?"

"Bucky, how are you, Bucky?"

"Son of a bitch. Globke. Rat bastard."

"Bucky, Bucky, Bucky."

"Who else but you. Money machine. Sitting behind your fat-ass desk."

"Bucky, Bucky."

"Why'd you turn this thing on? I don't want a telephone in here."

"Bucky, Bucky, Bucky."

"Shit machine. Rotten globke bastard. You globke son of a bitch. You're a fucking unspeakable adjective, you know that?"

"They can fix phones from the office. They did it from their office. The phone company. It wasn't broke, understand? It was just turned off. So we had them turn it on."

"Manager."

"You've suffered untold agony. You're distraught, you're bereaved, your stomach is extra-acidic. It's only natural you fling out in all directions. I understand this. I wouldn't have it any other way. Yell at me. Exhaust your vocabulary of foul words. I said to Lepp before I got into the car and picked up the phone to call you, I said to Lepp I'd rather have Bucky unload all the verbal garbage on me, his personal manager, instead of on top of the media, where it could hurt us a little bit. But the point is I'm sitting right now in this automobile of mine and I'm looking at the lights of the George Washington Bridge as I make my approach from the West Side Highway and I'm thinking it all means nothing to him. I'm thinking he's sitting there in this dead person's apartment suffering untold agony and for what? On the other side of this bridge is America. Do you hear what I'm saying, Bucky, above the whiz-whiz of the cars going the other way? America is out there, just beyond this bridge, and it's full of people who are waiting to be told what to do. Here I am on my way to a high-powered business dinner at Irv Koslow's Steak Fantasia in Metuchen and there you are suffering untold agony and for what? They want your sound out there. They want your words. They want your arms and legs and unmentionables. That's what I'm thinking as I sit here in this twenty-two-thousand-dollar banana boat of mine. I'm thinking other things too. I frankly admit that. I'm thinking dollar volume. I'm thinking grosses. I'm thinking unit sales. You can sit there for just so long. The best thing for you is work. The tour. The road. The travel. The tour represents a survival all its own, Bucky, and I know you perceive that truth. They're waiting out there, just the other side of this bridge. It's America. The whole big thing. Popcorn and killer drugs. You can't just sit there."

"You haven't sent Hanes down with any money lately."

"At least I got you thinking about money with that little speech of mine. The trouble is it's hard to get at it. We've got so many interlocking operations it's hard to know where to take from and who to give to. It's not easy to get at the money, Bucky. I'm trying to get at it. But so far nothing but legal hurdles. It's tied up, the money. It's being used to make more money. But I'm up on seven now and I've got the legal minds working on it. Our senior people. So maybe things might begin to loosen up and we can put you back on a cash-flow basis. Maybe not too. It's hard to get at. Everywhere I turn I run into a legal hurdle of one kind or another. Lepp meanwhile is running all over town planting trees to keep people happy because of all the demolitions he's got planned. There's real estate and unreal estate. Whoever's unhappy, Lepp plants trees. He tells them look how nice, a tree, a shrub, see how it makes up for the noise and monstrousness of tearing down an old building and putting up a new building. That's the whole secret of corporate structures, my friend. Tell the enemy you'll plant some trees."

"What do you want?" I said.

"It's not what I want, Bucky. It's what they want. The ones who buy what we sell. That's no life you're leading sitting in a dead person's room and I say these words as I cross the bridge right at this pivotal moment and prepare to go through the tollbooth to the first acre of real American soil where they're watching and waiting for either a return to your old self or the emergence of something new and chart-busting."

"I'm all through listening."

"Because this is a pivotal time in the music business and in the future of the country as a whole."

145

"Don't call back."

"Abuse me, I love it. Spit on my clothes, I'll never get them martinized. Nobody's happier than I am to dine in four-star restaurants with the spittle of a genius on my hand-tailored polyester checks. But one thing you should know about, Bucky."

"What's that?" I said.

"You were seen stealing a can of pineapple chunks in a supermarket in Fresno."

15

THE PACKAGE contained the mountain tapes. This was how Opel had chosen to mark the day of my birth.

On the tapes were twenty-three songs, all written and sung by me, all played by me (without accompaniment) on an old acoustic guitar, the first I'd ever owned. The songs were the most recent things I'd done. I'd taped them about fourteen months earlier, alone in the mountains, sitting down with the guitar and tape recorder and making up lyrics as I went along. I had just come off a world tour and my voice was weary and scorched, no sound nearer to my mind than the twang of baby murders in patriarchal hamlets. In time a visitor came upon the tapes and played them. Word got out, distorted of course, shaped by rumor and speculation. I refused to discuss the tapes with anyone. I declined to release them, to re-record the songs, to accept any offer concerning this material. I didn't understand the nature of my own labor. The guitar work was recognizable but the voice didn't seem to be mine. It possessed an extraordinary childlike blandness, a bit raw at times in its acknowledgments to pain, but mostly lone-some, homeless and dull, lacking true crudeness as well as any other distinctive quality. Beyond this were the lyrics themselves, strange little autistic ramblings. Perhaps because the words had never been put on paper, or even thought about for the briefest moment, these songs conveyed a special desolation, a kind of abnormal naturalness. In the past there had been a mind behind every babble and moan I'd ever produced. But the mountain tapes were genuinely infantile. I had no idea whether this was good or bad. I didn't know whether the songs were supposed to be redemptive, sardonic or something completely different. Tributes to my own mute following. Cheap plastic tricks. Ironic sonnets to the nation's crazed statesmen. Main Street parade noises. Commercials for baby food. Beseechings and calumets. Sequels to the ballads of the dead revolution. Whatever they were, the songs had come oozing out, one after another, over a period of two or three sleepless days. I had no clear memory of that period. The tapes themselves served as confirmation of what had taken place. Every reel was full of repetitions, mistakes and slurred words. There were long incoherent vocal passages interspersed with the sounds of eating, drinking and talking back to the TV. I played the tapes a number of times but their essence continued to elude me and so I simply put them away, preferring to forget what had been, after all, just a few days of unremembered effort — a collection of songs whose release would be sure to cause vast confusion. After that, mention of the tapes was made only by close friends or fetishistic rock scholars dressed like Superman.

I was younger then and felt an obligation to my audience. I wasn't fully aware of the uses to which confusion might be put. Fame is treble and bass, and only a rare man can command the dial to that fractional point where both tones are simultaneously his. Opel had put a murmur in my head. I didn't know when she had lifted the tapes from my house in the mountains and at first I thought she was being merely playful in returning them. Conjuring up my own past confusions. But of course there was more to it than that. I remembered several things she'd either said herself or instructed Hanes to say.

(1) The gift is a stroke of true bitch genius.

(2) It is to be referred to as the product.

(3) It is not to be opened until Globke starts maneuvering for his star's return.

Opel saw the tapes as my way back out. She'd known exactly what I needed. I'd told her my own designs were too evil for a mere dealer to understand. Now she was daring me to prove it, even giving me the means. Wunder's last lick. It was the chance to remake himself, lean man of mystery, returning with the fabled tapes for all to hear, luring his crowds to new silence, their fear in baby bottles under their seats. I didn't even have to create new material. That was part of the point of it all.

Watney called from the airport. He was on his way in to see me. England's anti-king and duplicate bishop of hallucination. Watney was in the fifth or sixth year of his semi-retirement. He'd done very few concerts and recordings in that time, preferring to study, meditate and gross millions. His sources of income were obscure and apparently varied. Money came to him in undetected torrents from the north of England, from the south of France, from secret places in the low wallowy bogs of Europe. When I asked him what he wanted to see me about, he said we'd have to discuss it in person. Man to man. Face to face. Hands across the table, as it were.

I repacked the tapes and put them back in the trunk. Opel's mind seemed present in the room. ("Evil is movement toward void.") I took off my shoes and socks, then sat on the bed and counted my toes. In not too long I'd be ready to learn firsthand what rages were ahead, boys and girls nibbling at my loins, season of gray space and unknowable words. Things to be figured out first, bits and pieces, some time to spend putting all together. I went into the bathroom and looked in the mirror, counting eyes, ears, nostrils and teeth.

16

WATNEY'S MANSERVANT Blessington was a portly boy with pink hands and the shuffling manner of someone who works in the subways. I watched him come up the stairs, four suitcases in his grasp and an airline bag around his neck. Watney followed, wearing blue suede shoes. He shook my hand, looked around the room and took the chair near the window, sniffing once through each nostril. Blessington sat on the floor amid luggage.

"We've got a limousine all right," Watney said. "It's parked right downstairs. Three rooms and a dining alcove. But at the same time fairly inconspicuous. Black. Solid black. Black inside and out. See, I wanted something inconspicuous. That's the way I like to travel. No point in being ostentatious. Given the two choices, inconspicuous or ostentatious, I would never hesitate past the natural reaction time for making a pointblank decision. But you're wondering why I've had the luggage brought upstairs. We've got a limousine all right. But I didn't want the luggage getting nicked. That's it then. I didn't want some rampant New York junkie ripping off my accumulated luggage. You see, the car's all right. The car's got a driver inside. We didn't trust the driver with the luggage. But we trust him with the car. That's his job, innit? The luggage is mine. The car is his. We trust him to look after the car."

"What's the noise in England?" I said.

"Haven't been there for a while. I'm headed there next. I'm coming from the other way, you see. Sneaking up on the notorious Bucky Wunderlick from an unlikely direction. Your manager gave me the details of your whereabouts and every single digit of your phone number. So I says to myself I shall ring him from the airport this very second. He's a decent sort he is, your Globke. Shut up, twit."

"What, me?" Blessington said. "I'm ultra-silent all this while."

"I anticipate your digressions."

"I'm sitting here quiet-like minding the bags. I'm sitting here like I used to sit in me own mum's sitting room. We used to sit we did. Two of us. Her with her pint. Me flashing me privates at the telly. Two of us. Sitting in the sitting room."

"I could have gone back direct," Watney said. "But instead I flew down from Toronto for a visit with my brother musician. Not that I'm flogging the old Gretsch too often. I'm into sales, procurement and operations now. I represent a fairly large Anglo-European group. That's my predominant area of interest. That's where I get my leverage. I still do the odd concert, you know. Keep my hand in, all that. But not like the old days when they drove us city to city like bloody oxen. It was crazy then, wunnit?"

"Still is," I said.

"I remember America. Touring the states. That was something then. That was the pinnacle of insanity. Everybody was crazy. They were all crazy."

"It hasn't changed that much."

"We got stuck in new levels of madness every day. All over the country there was nothing but madness. America was the sheer peak. They were all crazy one way or another. It was guns, sex and politics. It was dope and color. It was motorcycles, garbage and hand-to-hand fighting. The one thing I couldn't take was polluting the environment. In England we've got a man who sees to that."

"Did you get to California this trip?"

"Did Canada this trip. It was an all-Canada operation. Laying some groundwork. Feeling things out. New territory more or less. No, missed California this trip. Good friends out there. Out there's different. I liked California. Not the same kind of edgy pace."

"They drink human blood," I said.

"But the weather," he said. "Fantastic streak of weather last time."

"They tear the entrails out of dogs and cats and offer them up as devotions to dead movie stars."

"The weather's the thing out there. I remember the weather."

"California weather," I said.

"That's it, California weather. That's just how I'd describe it myself. Good friends in L.A. Nordquist and that lot. Kept getting busted. He came to London, you know, Nordquist did. Got busted right off. They had him sewing mailbags. He went to Sweden after that. Bang, got put right into one of their experimental prisons. You can fuck on the grounds and all. Good friends in L.A."

"The sun shines right through the night."

"That's the feeling you get, innit? That's the mental picture the whole scene brings to mind."

"Warm and bright and never rains."

"That's it," he said.

"They eat their offspring. They have multimedia human sacrifices. Records, tapes, films, light shows, puppet shows, blinking neon drugstore signs, copulating farm animals. People devour their own babies."

In the days of his fame Watney had been able to work a mean streak into the nerve centers of entire cities. His band was called Schicklgruber and wherever they went the village elders consulted local ordinances trying to find a technicality they might use to keep the band from performing or at the very least to get the band out of town the moment the last note sounded. Watney played an icy guitar, enticing his sounds through merciless progressions. Bitch-picking, he called it. But Schicklgruber's true impact was extramusical. Watney ranged across the stage, primed to a tailored flash, his costume derived from leotards one night, pedal pushers the next, outrageous in the parodies he devised. This was his art, to take a tiny stitch and rip it wide, blinking while the blood flowed, society's uncoiled parts left without their package. The band didn't arouse the violent appetites of the young as much as it killed all appetite, causing a dazed indifference to just about everything. Watney wrote his lyrics in the back seats of limousines.

"I'm a buyer. But sometimes I sell. I'm a buyer who sometimes sells. That's where I get my leverage. We've got footholds in a number of places. We're Anglo-European by and large. Fulfillment. See, that's the thing I'm after. I wasn't getting my fulfillment with music. It's like everybody's got a fulfillment quota and mine wasn't being satisfied. I had no real power in the music structure. It was all just show. This thing about my power over kids. Watney the transatlantic villain. Schicklgruber the assassin of free will. It was just something to write, to fill up the newspapers with. I had no power, Bucky. I just dollied about on stage with my patent leather pumps and my evil leer. It was a good act all right. But it was all just an act, just a runaround, just a show. So now I'm doing sales and procurements and operations and I'm here to bid on the product you're holding."

"You're doing more than operations," I said. "You're running the thing, aren't you?"

"It's a question of territories, see. I hold up the British end. I run the British side of things."

"What things?"

"Right now the biggest item is the microdot. The microdot is definitely number one at the moment. Our choicest item. It's going faster than we can replenish our supply. Of course you get the odd fatality with microdots. You get the odd jumper-off-a-bridge or runner-into-speeding-train. That's what gives microdots their bad name. The stuff makes you want to dash across the tracks into a speeding train. Fear and terror, terror and fear. These elements are at the very heart of the human drama. Eh, Blessington? Read your Kafka. Read your bloody Orwell. The state creates fear through force. The state uses force eight thousand miles away in order to create fear at home. Do you know what NTBR means?"

"No," I said.

"Blessy, do you know what NTBR means?"

"Me mum never taught me the alphabet."

"NTBR means not to be resuscitated. Certain patients in certain hospitals throughout England are marked NTBR. These patients include the elderly, the malignant and the chronic. In the event of heart stoppage, such patients are left un-re-suss-ee-tay-ted. What's your opinion of this practice? Speak into the microphone please."

"My opinion of this practice," Blessington said. "Is that the question?"

"Submoronic twit."

"I love England I do. I will never say a word against her."

"Does NTBR mark the true beginning of the killer state?"

"Tell me what to say and I'll say it."

"Slobber, don't you, when the piercing questions are asked. Cringe and snivel in the face of the heavy pressures. A dim thing, Blessy, that's what you be. Slow. All too bloody slow."

"Prenatal malnutrition," Blessington said.

"You've long since tipped the balance the other way, haven't you, piggeldy-wiggeldy?"

"Don't you go insulting me again."

"A right rosy piglet you are. Ready for the spit."

"Don't you go saying that now. I'll hold my breath I will. Then you'll be sorry. Then you'll see the error of your ways."

"Turning, turning, turning. Burning, burning, burning. Melting in the mouth like fresh farm butter."

"You'll go too far one day. The way mum went too far

156

with poor old dad every time dad sat himself in the sitting room to read the adverts. You'll give me a stroke you will. How would you like it if I had a stroke that paralyzed one side of my body? Who would cook for you and see to your luggage and clean the house and offer unstinting companionship?"

"The other side of your body," Watney said.

"Poo on you, mate."

"Back to the question at hand. Given the choice, Blessy, would you rather be an elderly, a malignant or a chronic? Into the microphone if you would."

"My solicitor instructs me to say nothing at this time."

"Crafty little brute. He's a crafty little brute, this one is. We have our small entertainments, Bucky. You're all done with traveling but we're still inveterate travelers. We have to have our entertainments. We need something to while away the time, we inveterates of the travel game. Is the product in this room, Bucky? If not, why not?"

"Which product is that?"

"I'm here to make a serious bid," Watney said. "We Anglo-Europeans are serious businessmen. We cling to the old methods, the old ways, the old traditions. None of your slick trading here. We make a solid offer and we stick to it. We are solid business people. We have various interests and a vast number of operations. We aren't larky boys out for a bit of a punch-up. We're after money, not thrills. Our operations are solid operations. We don't use unorthodox methods and we don't employ maniacs, sadists and addicts. This is our way. The orthodox way. The Anglo-European way."

"Tell him about the Malta deal," Blessington said.

17

IN THE NIGHT I passed people trooping home with their newspapers, bearers of a weight that went beyond simple pounds and ounces. They headed up a street still blistered with neon and other watery sores, men and women almost single file, leaning into the wind, mountain guides trained against complaint, hired to carry home this swollen load and undress it section by section until the only thing left was the blur of faint print on their fingers. Against the moral obligations of their Saturday night, only yards from the newsstand, they had to walk around a man burning wooden crates, standing almost in the fire, looking at no one, a man dressed in a black coat with pockets torn away, leaving streaks of white lining at his hips. I held my hands for a moment over the flames. The man's own hands were furled in each other, held high on his chest, fingernails of rust and chiseled silver, half-moon scar, shredded skin at the knuckles, luxuriant gash the length of one thumb. Easy to imagine a hundred miles of lines crosshatching his palms. Covering the man's head was a football helmet, Miami Dolphins, complete with face mask.

"Retractable ball points," he said. "Thirty-five cents."

Down Second Avenue, darker here in its plodding Ukrainian sleep, I saw a small woman about to cross the street. She pointed at the opposite corner, holding her right arm perfectly straight, index finger extended. Then she lowered the arm and walked swiftly across the street in the direction she'd indicated. Here she made a sharp left turn, raised her arm, pointed over the speckled concrete to the end of the block and walked in that direction. Turn, point, march. I watched her stop at the far corner, turn to the right and point again. A Good Humor truck, stripped and gutted, sat in a lot near the Bowery. I walked slowly west. For a second nothing moved. There were no people in sight and traffic was nonexistent. I stopped on the corner and looked all around me. The wind took papers and boxes. Then, finally, about two blocks south, I saw men with rags go out into the middle of the street to await the next cycle of traffic, men with rags to clean the windshields, going out slowly from doorways and side streets, clean the windshields for a fee, men limping into the street, about a dozen of them, and then the first car came into view, moving north from one of the bridges or from Chinatown or Little Italy or the bank buildings, the first car followed by others, their lights rising over humps in the street, scores of cars coming up the Bowery toward the wild men with rags.

Micklewhite's door was open. The frame and edge of the door had been splintered. I looked into the room. She was sitting on a sofa watching television. I knocked on the door frame and she looked up.

"I told them go scratch your ass with a broken bottle. Go scratch your heinie, I told them. I wasn't afraid of them. Them or nobody else. Breaking in my door like that and coming in here to smack me around. I don't take that. Don't come in here and give me that. I ain't afraid of you punks and bums. I told them, mister. I don't take smacking around. You want to rob me, one thing. Smack me around, whole different thing. My husband was here, they'd see. He'd of cut them up good. I'm telling you, mister. Good thing for them he's dead and buried."

"How many?" I said.

"There was four come in here and some more out in the hall that never even made it in. Smash, they come right through the door. Then when they got out of here they went upstairs, the whole bunch. I heard them on three, making noise with the mister up on three. Breaking through the door, smash. Crazy people. Say nothing, do nothing, take nothing. Crumbums, I told them, go scratch your heinie."

"Did they hurt you?"

"It was him that stopped them," she said. "They seen him there and that stopped them cold. He was right there on the chair and when they seen that, they went charging upstairs, taking over the whole building. They came in here to smack me around. Then they seen him on the chair and they went flying out. Good thing for them I got no more husband. He was good and sneaky in a fight. He was just a skinny-melink but he made up for it with sneakiness. Little as he was he'd sneak-fight bigger men right into the crash ward. He'd jap them when they weren't ready. He'd go for the family jewels. That was the only thing in the world he was good at. Japping bigger men. He put many a bigger man out of commission. Sneakiest s.o.b. you'd ever want to meet."

I stepped into the room. Her son was on a chair in the corner. His own special chair, it seemed. No upholstery. Wood frame, binding, springs, two bed pillows. He wasn't sitting or reclining; he was stored there, his head slowly rolling side to side, arms and legs stunted. Because of his disfigurement, everything about him was pervasively real and I was struck by a panic that went far beyond what my eyes had registered. His face seemed to have the consistency of pounded mud. The head was full of bulges and incurvatures, scant of hair, a soft curious object that seemed to belong in a greenish jar. Useless pair of clubhands. Arms about three-quarters normal size. Legs perhaps less than that. The boy was unforgettable in the sheer organic power of his presence. Standing before him was like witnessing the progress of some impossible mutation, bird to brown worm, but of course he'd been merely deposited there, wet, white and unchanging, completely stagnant, and I began to feel that I myself was the other point of the progression. The sense of shock and panic hadn't left me yet and I understood why the marauders were not eager to browse in this particular room. One felt nearly displaced by the hint of structural transposition; he was what we'd always feared, ourselves in radical divestment, scrawled across the dark. Instead of leaving I went closer, drawn into what I felt was his ascendancy, the helpless strength of his entrapment in tepid flesh, in the reductions of being. I lowered myself to one knee and sought to trace some sightline or bearing in his pale stare. With my left hand I raised his head, finding nothing in the eyes beyond a rhythmic blink. I must have seemed a shadow to him, thin liquid, incidental to the block of light he lived in. For the first time I began to note his embryonic beauty. The blank eyes ticked. The mouth opened slightly, closing on loomed mucus. I'd thought the fear of being peeled to this limp circumstance had caused my panic, the astonishment of blood pausing in the body. But maybe it was something else as well, the possibility that such a circumstance concludes in beauty. There was a lure to the boy, an unsettling lunar pull, and I moved my hand over the moist surface of his face. Beauty is dangerous in narrow times, a knife in the slender neck of the rational man, and only those who live between the layers of these strange days can know its name and shape. When I took my hand from his face, the head resumed its metronomic roll. I was still afraid of him, more than ever in fact, but willing now to breathe his air, to smell the bland gases coming off him, to work myself into his consciousness, whatever there was of that. It would have been better (and even cheering) to think of him as some kind of super-crustacean or diabolic boiled vegetable. But he was too human for that, adhering to me as though by suction or sticky filaments. Mouth opened and closed. Eyes blinked at precise intervals. Head moved from side to side. Micklewhite adjusted the sound on her TV set.

"Careful, he bites," she said.

I went upstairs to see Fenig. The door was almost off, leaning from the lower hinge. He was seated at his typewriter, looking into the keys. Bandages, tape and gauze were all over the floor. He tapped out a few characters, then turned toward the door and gave me a small wave. His face was full of bruises. There were bloodstains all over his clothes. Both brows were puffed up, his lower lip cut open, thick with dried blood. He hadn't applied bandages or gauze to his wounds, at least not in exposed areas. I stood there watching him type a line or two, very slowly, his fingers merely pecking at the keys prior to each actual assault, the moment in which the words moved through his hands and found the page. He looked my way a second time.

"Magazines keep folding. It's not so good. I've spent a lot of time lately worrying about whether or not I've lost the essential spark. It's not me I should have been concerned about. It's the market. The market is getting smaller every day. The bright lights are dimming. The sounds and echoes are fading. The great elliptical arc is spinning ever slower."

"Did they take anything?" I said.

"They just cuffed me around and stomped me a little bit. I was lucky. They were in the room probably only sixty seconds. They made a lot of noise coming up the stairs and a lot of noise going back down the stairs. I think that was the biggest part of their operation. The idea of taking over a building. The idea of breaking and entering. The idea of domination. It could have been a whole lot worse. I was lucky. I can't get over how lucky I was. I know people who'd give almost anything to be as lucky as I was."

"Do you want me to help you clean up this mess?"

"You mean the bandages and stuff. I'm the one who flung the bandages and stuff. They didn't do that. I'm the one who did that. After they left I got all this stuff out of my medicine chest. The Band-Aid plastic strips. The safety gauze. The nonstick sterile pads. The first-aid tape. The absorbent cotton. I got it all out. I laid it out on the table and looked at it. I looked especially hard at the tan bandages with the clever little air vents. Then I swept the whole thing right off the table. What good's gauze and cotton against the idea of domination? What good's a sterile compress against the idea of domination? So I'll bleed. So I'll experience discomfort for a few days. I don't think about that because right now, as I sit in this chair talking to you, I'm in the midst of work on a whole new genre. Fi-nance. Financial writing. Books and articles for millionaires and potential millionaires. The floodgates are opened and the words are pouring out. Financial literature. Handled right it's a goddamn gold mine, relatively speaking."

My own door had not been touched. I went inside and turned on the radio. It was cold in the room. There was an airline bag near the door, accidentally left behind by Watney's manservant. The phone rang. It was Azarian in Los Angeles, saying his people were very anxious to bid. I hung up. On the radio several men were conversing in an unfamiliar language. I looked in the trunk for an extra blanket. The package containing the mountain tapes was gone. I had to work my way up and down several mental steps before I arrived at this conclusion. I knew at once that something was missing from the trunk. I realized it was the brown package. I thought the package contained the drug. Then I remembered Hanes had the package with the drug. The second package contained the tapes. The second package was gone. I stood in a corner of the room, near the window, crossing and uncrossing my arms, finally wedging my hands in my armpits for warmth. I knew I'd never be able to reproduce the complex emotional content of those tapes, or remember a single lyric.

After a while I went over to the door, picked up Watney's airline bag and unzipped it. Inside were several hundred bubble gum cards. Watney's picture was on each one of them. A funny enough sight. But not what I needed at the moment.

There was no extra blanket. I put Opel's coat over my shoulders, placed the one available blanket over the coat and then settled into a chair and waited for the first line of light to appear across the window, bringing sleep with no dreams.

18

I PICKED UP the telephone and listened to the dial tone, music of a dead universe. The sound fascinated me. Ever since the phone had been put back in working order, I had fallen into the habit of lifting the receiver from time to time and simply listening. Source of pleasure and fear never before explored. It was always the same, silence endowed with acoustical properties.

I dialed the numbers of Globke's office, his home, his car. Nobody knew where he was. His wife spoke to me about the stillness at the center of a thing in motion. In the background, as she talked, I heard my own voice, revolving at thirty-three and a third, second cut on side one of third album.

A man wearing a gendarme's cape appeared at the door. He was small and pallid, almost lost in the cape and long boots, and in his eyes was a frenzy he seemed to be trying to pass off as alertness. He gestured toward the bathroom.

"What's in there?"

"Everything that's not in here."

"My name isn't important. Menefee. It happens to be Menefee but that's not important. What's important is the person I'm clearing for. I'm here to clear. I'm here to make the area secure before you and the person in question conduct your undisclosed business. We have procedures we've developed over a long period of time. Can I use your phone?"

As he dialed he stood between me and the telephone. Talking to the person at the other end he buried his head in the cape. Merely listening he turned slightly and glanced my way every few seconds, as if verifying a description.

"Change of plan," he said. "We don't go there. He comes here."

"Who comes here?" I said.

"Dr. Pepper."

"He's going to be disappointed."

"Don't tell me anything," Menefee said. "I'm only here to clear. I make things secure. I work with details, not sum totals. I don't want to be made a party to any information that has sum totals involved in it. This job is tough enough. Handling details for a man like Dr. Pepper is like the ultimate in nerve-rackingness. We run up and down the country, in and out of hotels, motels, airplanes, taxicabs. Seeing people, fleeing people. Making deals, turning wheels. Dr. Pepper is a master of many things. People think he restricts his genius to dope and matters related to dope. Dope-related matters. Not so. The man shows his genius in an unspecified number of ways, each and every day, north and south, in lake country or mountain terrain, talking to the makers and shakers or just ambling along a country road laying a gentle rap on some backpacker who's

167

into penance and mortification. But the man's a stickler for detail and this makes my work tough as can be. Soon's we get something all set up he contacts me in some devious way and changes eight details out of a possible eleven. You could say the man's hyper-secretive. You could use adjectives like eerie and uncanny and you'd be right on the mark. He's got disguises, he's got surprises. He doesn't trust a soul, least of all me. He's all the time devising tests to determine my loyalty. The man's a master of regional accents, a master of total recall, a master of surreptitiousness. Every time I meet some stranger somewhere I automatically assume it's Dr. Pepper in disguise probing at my loyalty. But the man's an aw-thentic genius. I'm grateful to him. I had two years of crisis sociology at the University of California at Santa Barbara in Santa Barbara, California. Ruined my head just about. Dr. Pepper took me out of the world of terminology and numbers and classifications and provided access to new kinds of awareness. Centrifugalism and overloads. Brain-patching. Electrode play areas."

He stopped talking abruptly and I became aware of a jackhammer beating into the street about half a block to the west. I sat at the small table near the sink. Menefee remained by the door, his body yielding to an occasional mild twitch, his face reflecting a mental concentration so intense I thought his eyeballs might suddenly click backward in their sockets in order to peer into the depths of his mind, leaving curdled sludge and pink drippings for my own eyes to gaze upon. Slowly he moved across the door, opened it an inch and looked into the hall. Then he billowed back toward the middle of the room, followed by the man himself, Dr. Pepper, a figure of ordinary size, wearing ordinary and somewhat out-of-date clothing, all in all no less common than a clam on a paper plate. Menefee made clearing motions with his hands and after the door was locked, the shade drawn and the introductions made, we crowded around the table, Pepper and I seated on identical straight-backed chairs and facing each other, Menefee between us in the low-slung canvas chair, leaning forward, his face at table level.

"The product isn't here," I said.

"I've been apprised of that," Dr. Pepper said. "This courier they hired is off somewhere trying to deal on his own. Predictable. At the very least semi-predictable. This Happy Valley bunch is not what you'd call a heads-up collection of people. They've got initiative to spare but they lack keenness. First they tell me to expect two people with the product. Then there's an unforeseeable delay. In my lexicon there's only one kind of delay. Strategic delay. But I let it pass without comment although I'm satisfied in my own mind, see, that this bunch lacks the necessary keenness. You hone yourself. I've honed myself over the years. I've dealt with the quickest minds and the quickest intellects. That's how I've acquired my own quickness. I've dealt with people who know which deck is the marked deck. I call these people the makers and shakers. You hone yourself. You cut away the glut. So then what do they tell me? They tell me the messenger is now bargaining agent with full bargaining powers. I replace the phone with a smile. A smile creases my face. Lack of judgment, I conclude. Lack of experience. In other words Happy Valley is not to be trusted. Their leadership is not to be trusted. Their hirelings and minions are not to be trusted. Other agencies of the underground are to be viewed with a jaundiced eye in the light of past performance. U.S. Guv is to be viewed with two such eyes in light of the fact that they're the victims of this rip-off. I have one word for U.S. Guv. Booshit. That word is booshit. What is U.S. Guv? It's a bunch of rich men playing golf. It's big business, big army and big government all visiting each other in company planes for the sole purpose of playing golf and talking money. So who does that leave in positions of trust? Friend, it leaves you and me."

Dr. Pepper wore a small fedora with the brim turned down. His suit was a couple of sizes too large, an aged gray outfit over a narrow gray and white tie and a dingy white shirt with frayed collar. He appeared to be in his late forties. His face was blank, tending toward narrowness, and his eyes were dark and still. Although at first he seemed unremarkable in every way, I began to note touches of professionalism about him. His deadpan expression was classically intact, put together from a strip of silent film, frame by frame. His speech was flat and rickety, hard-working in its plainness, the voice of an actor delivering monologues from a rocking chair. Of course I had the advantage of knowing who he was. Also I was fairly certain I'd seen him before and heard either that voice or an approximation. Perhaps the oddest thing about Dr. Pepper was that he didn't wear glasses. He had the kind of face that needed glasses to be complete, old rimless spectacles worn low on the nose, but the absence of this final detail only confirmed his elusiveness and skill; one was inclined to fill in the face, provide a finish to the comic proposition. A single thing connected all others — the invisible mannerisms, the craft, the tightfisted humor — and this one threading element was danger. Dr. Pepper had lived among dangerous men, worked in hazardous circumstances, and his eccentricity, his distance from the axis, had its origins in the basic machine-like pressures that bear on a man who is unable to think or live in accordance with the central themes of the law. Even his appearance, ordinary as it was, suggested some acquaintance with illegality. More than anything else he looked like a man released from prison in 1947 in Joliet, Illinois. It would have been difficult to say what crime he'd been convicted for. He had the gift of putting distance between himself and his applauders. My own tenuous guesses would have included child-molesting, embezzlement, the defrauding of widows.

"I'll tell you, Buck. This stuff they've come up with is not the kind of product a man like me is likely to dismiss. I give them points for initiative. I have sources and these sources confirm what I've long suspected. This isn't some kind of rinky-dink schoolboy caper. No way, manner, shape or form. This is a weighty affair we're involved in here. This drug is some kind of extreme substance. This is a pressing matter and deserves our closest attention."

"I've figured that out for myself," I said. "Everybody in the free world wants to bid. There's a group on the Coast wants to bid. They're very anxious to bid. There's a group in Europe also wants to bid, also very anxious. That's Watney's group. Great Britain and Europe. I haven't heard from the Japanese yet. Of course Hanes may have heard. He's out there with the product."

"Watney first swam into my ken in Boston," Dr. Pepper said. "Sure, Watney and that crowd of his. I was bumping into a whole lot of crank behavior about then. There was a man there that could imitate a sewing machine. There was a pair of girls, Lenore and Doreen, they come up from right off the street, quack-quack, sisters they were, Lenore's the fat one, see, and they're trying to sell me a radio that gets Perth, Australia. I'd just finished manufacturing and dealing off I won't say how many dollars worth of shiny black capsules in bulk, posing as my own sales manager. There were any number of stunts being pulled that night. The sewing machine guy was being hypnotized by a cousin of Watney's that was making his first trip here and refused to leave the hotel for fear of being lashed to the fender of a car and taken north for resale to a lumber operation. At that time in Boston stories of abduction in the night were rife. There was a guy there as I recall, Montaldo, a promoter and manager who on the side controlled the entire orchid business north of Braintree right up to the border, for whatever that's worth. Watney himself was tripping in a unique and interesting manner. There was a kitchenette in the place, just the bare essentials, and Watney takes an egg and places it whole and intact on a frying pan, no fire going, no heat coming up, and he stands there waiting for a fried egg to appear and he just can't understand why it won't. Nobody knew who I was. I was drifting through the suite, witness to any number of propositions. The equipment man for some local group, name of Mulderick, I recall, he's selling credit cards, driver's licenses, army discharge papers, transcripts from Harvard Business School. A kid with his arm in a cast tells me the cast has a secret compartment for transporting dope and offers me the plans for twenty dollars. I'm diverted by all these signs of enterprise. I find it an occasion of mild diversion with the sole and single exception of the hypnotism routine which I can tell is being done without any real feel for the subject, which is a subject I happen to know something about, being the recipient of one of the few legitimate degrees in hypnotology ever given out by an accredited college in this country. Watney by this time has placed a call to his house outside London and finds himself in the regrettable situation of not being at home to answer the telephone. He's trying to call himself, ding-ding, and nobody's picking up the phone. The result is fear and dread. He sits on the floor weeping real tears into the phone. Oh, it's a crisis of no small proportion. The guy is in the grip of blackest anxiety. Absolute terror in his eyes. Oh, he's terror-stricken, no doubt about it, ding-ding-ding in his ear. This was Watney when he first swam into my ken, long before he picked up the shield of the businessman."

"Tell me if I'm right," I said. "You were here the night there was a party here. Whole place full of people. You smoked a pipe. You were the professor of latent history. You talked about that a while. Tell me if I'm right about that."

"I'll tell you why I was here, Buck. I was here to check on the young lady's credentials. At that point I didn't know the product was in your possession. But I did know the identity of Happy Valley's chief agent. So being I was in town and being I knew about the little shindig through various local sources, I thought I'd drop on by. I wanted to make the young lady's acquaintance, get the first foothold in the bargaining process. Unhappily, never got to say a word to her. She retired early, faded away in the midst of all that smoke."

"I remember."

"Just scouting out the premises. I like to do that, earliest opportunity. Same as I was doing when you and I first met."

"We met the same night you came to meet Opel."

"Earlier," he said. "I knew you'd been in touch with Happy Valley. Wanted to scout out the whole neighborhood, including your place. Just a quick look around, swish-swish, in and out, to get my bearings."

"When was this?"

"I was the brush salesman. I came around with a sample case and some patter about mutilation and exchange rates."

"Gaw-damn."

"An old, a very old routine of mine. Thought I'd dust it off and try it, being I was here in town."

"I was told you didn't travel anymore," I said.

"I'll tell you how word got out on that. I leaked that particular word. Have to keep people off balance. If you let people maintain their balance, there's any number of things likely to happen, the likeliest of which is that you lose the edge. Operations of this kind are a matter of balance and edge. I still travel. I like slipping in and out. Like coming to New York four, five times a year."

"Not me," Menefee said. "I have to load up on dope every time we come to New York. I stoke myself like a coal-burning engine. New York is too real. It's just about the realest thing there is in the observable universe."

"We're growing a race of giants here," I said. "This fact isn't clear yet but will be one day soon. Men, women and children. All giants. Prepared to eat glass and punch their way through concrete."

"I stoke up, man. I mix me some weird concoctions. That's the only way I can survive this kind of realness."

"I like traveling close to the ground," Dr. Pepper said. "Getting to know the road people. The drifters. The pure products. I can recall Roy Best, a legendary banjo player who was working for a perforating company when I ran across him. Bushwick Perforating, Roy Best. Another legend about that time was Vincent T. Skinner, habitué of the billiard parlors, a whole anthropological culture in itself, Vinny Skinny, sold pool tables door to door because he loved the game, Vincent T. Skinner, froze to death in the middle of summer when he went to sleep in a refrigerated packing house between shifts. Mylon Ware, the mad dog folk singer, a near legend. James Radley, nutritionist, a legend many times over. The semi-legendary disc jockey, Howard Mud Stump Meegan, a man who wore white socks every day of his life because his feet were allergic to colored dyes. Bobby Boy Todd, a free spirit who worked as a dispatcher for a bus company, dispatching buses until he quit to travel, just travel, nothing but travel, spent his days and nights traveling, a free spirit, a legend of travel, married a half-breed girl and on his wedding day fractured both legs riding a kid's tricycle down a ravine. Why are free spirits always so fucking dumb? Rosalee Dowdy, the comic book queen, a legend and a half. Tristan Bramble, folklorist and musicologist, busted for possession nine times, an important early influence. Earlene Griffin, the r-and-b arranger, a seminal figure. Just last night at the Port Authority Bus Terminal where I like to hang out when I'm in New York, I ran into Vernon Kliegl and Mary Kliegl, the husband and wife midgets who became legends in the late fifties for department store pilferage. They're more or less retired now, living on deferred income. Stone drunk when I ran into them. Hanging all over each other. I called them but they were too drunk to hear me. So I followed them toward the down escalator. The down escalator as it turns out was not running at all, out of order, stalled. The Kliegls are standing there on the top step, too drunk to know they're not moving. The up escalator is working fine and about a hundred people go gliding past the Kliegls before Mary Kliegl realizes they've been stationary all this while and begins punching Vernon Kliegl on the arm and chest, demanding to know what the hell is going on. A smile creases my face. I choose this moment to get them off the escalator. Vernon recognizes me right away and we shake hands and start talking about this and that. I'm aware all the while we're talking that Mary Kliegl is looking up at me and squinting, too drunk to know who I am. She resumes her battering of Vernon's arm and chest, all the time squealing out at him: *Who is that, who is he, do we know him?* I finally had to cut the conversation short for the sake of Vernon Kliegl's physical well-being. She wouldn't even let me explain who I was. Midgets are clannish people."

His hands were set flat on the table. All through the narrative there was no change in his expression. I knew those people were out there. The pure so-called products. Found dead near railroad tracks or shipped in bulk to the warehouses of the certifiably insane. Pepper nevertheless seemed to be reciting for mere exercise. Maybe he was giving this particular identity a workout, stretching its muscles, adding a furlong to its distance. To my ear there were no defects in the unstressed delivery of his voice.

"What happens now?" I said.

"Eventually I want to package the stuff in twenty-five-milligram green capsules. Mean green beans. Too early to work out pricing."

"But you don't have the sample. Hanes has it."

"That's why I'm here, Buck. Hanes won't be able to unload the product easy as all that. Hanes doesn't know about balance and edge. The kid's untried and untested, a pissy little babe among the timber wolves. He doesn't have any up-top connections and he doesn't know what it's like out there, although by this time he's maybe finding out. He'll be back is my guess. He can't stay out there indefinitely without putting himself in grave danger. This whole business qualifies as high risk. If he survives at all, back here is the first place he'll come. I'm all but convinced of that. He'll put the thing back where he got it from. That's the first instinct of the trapped man. Meanwhile I'll be close by. I'll be keeping an eye on things. I'll be in touch."

"I may not be here," I said.

"Buck, I want this product badly. This may be my last venture in the field of drugs and drug abuse. I crave new frontiers. There's a craving in my breast for the uncharted spaces and territories of the human mind. Energy. I want to tap untapped fields of energy. Dope is okay. Dope is the power of the earth, the use of earth products to dig deeper into the earthen parts of the mind. But energy is the power of the universe. I want to tap that power. I see masses of people changing their energy patterns by controlling biorhythms from the basic frequencies of the universe. Stereo electrodes. Control of internal changes. I envision abuses, of course. I envision mail-order ads in the rear extremities of men's magazines. Cures cancer in seconds! Adds inches to your cock! But that kind of booshit's inevitable and I can't take time to worry about it, much as it grieves me in the professional sense. I'm already semi-involved in a process I call the process of centrifugalism. Stereo electrodes. Blood-pressure impactors. What I call the auto-domination of the inner mind."

"I've got problems right now that don't have anything to do with you or Hanes or the universe."

"I want to end this phase of my career with a technical and merchandising feat that goes beyond the legendary. You and I, friend, are the only two people in positions of trust. Once the product is returned, we'll go into deep consultation. Where there's money to be made and legends to be created, I don't leave anything to chance and it strikes me as boding well for the future of our partnership that you've been wooed by other agencies of the underground without releasing the product. But accept a word of caution. This operation is fraught with danger. Bohack is not a man to be trifled with. He's an edgy gent with all kinds of deliveries. Some reasonable. Some not so."

"Who the hell is Bohack?"

"Pffff."

"What?" I said.

"He laughed," Menefee said. "That's the way he laughs. Pffff. Pffff-pffff. It took me months before I caught on. For months I thought he was blowing loose threads off my shirt."

In his toxic glee Menefee repeatedly bumped his chin on the edge of the table. Finally he told me that Bohack was the name of the man who commanded one of Happy Valley's two camps. As both men rose I heard the pneumatic drill jabbing into stone. Then Dr. Pepper took a pair of glasses from the inside pocket of his suit coat. With a disposable tissue he rubbed the lenses, held them to the light and then carefully fitted the glasses over his ears and nose. They were dark glasses with heavy black frames. A touch of comic paranoia, I thought. One disguise covering another. The touring clown doubly self-effaced.

19

Opel and I made love once in the anechoic chamber in the mountains. I thought of this as I lay in bed, unable to sleep. What were we like then, in that time and space, unburdened of the weight of outer sound? We were like angels harboring each other in the notion of desirelessness, dazed in our acquiescence to this drift through subatomic matter. The love of minds should last beyond lives. Maybe it does, each mind a dice-toss of neutron stars, invisible except to theory, pulling at cold space to find its lover. Opel never returned to the chamber because the wedge-shaped baffles made her think of bats hanging in a cave.

I took the number of steps necessary to get from the bed to the door. No one was there. I picked up a magazine and tried to read a column of print, getting to the second line before I had to stop because of the pressure behind my eyes. Molten water dripped from the pipe connected to the radiator, bleaching the wood floor. It was almost daylight, snow on the way, the phone squatting on the stacked phone books, the firemen breathing in the firehouse. I went to the door again. A young black woman stood in the hall, legs well apart, hands on hips. She was arrayed in burnishings and pleated streaks, and there was a trim glitter about her, a commercial grace, evident in the seamless way she shifted weight to orchestrate a sort of stylish body violence. I stood there in old shorts and dirty toenails. Azarian came up the stairs then. We went inside, where he took a chair and I got into bed. The woman remained in the open doorway. For the first time in three days I felt it was possible to sleep.

"The group broke up," Azarian said. "As a group we no longer exist. We officially broke up."

"Who's the nice lady?"

"Security," he said. "Her name's Epiphany Powell. Maybe you've heard of her. She used to sing, she used to model, she used to act. Now she's doing security. The group broke up. We no longer exist as a group. Of course there wasn't any real hope once you left. Still and all it's frightening. Nobody was really prepared for it. But it happened. We no longer exist in the old sense."

"As of when?"

"I heard it on the radio coming in from the airport. When I left L.A., things were still in flux. Nothing was decided to the point where we could come out and say we've reached a decision. But I guess we broke up because I heard it on the radio. It sounded pretty official. Who has final word in these matters?"

"The radio," I said.

"A lot of it was my doing," he said. "I got heavily involved in black music. Not performing or producing. Just listening. That old showcase stuff with everybody in shiny clothes and pomaded hair. Brushed drums, piano, sax breaks. 'Baby don't you know that I love you so.' I'm into that sound, Bucky, and I can't get out. After all these years I realize that's the only sound I really love. So I neglected the band and now we no longer exist as a group. The little dance routines they do. Hands flashing out, feet gliding, bodies whirling so smoothly. Romantic soul music done by immortal groups. The Infatuations. The Tailfins. The Splendifics. 'It's a hurtin' pain you give me, babe, but I'm fightin' for my love.' It's all love and sorrow, Bucky, and it just about destroys me emotionally. The crude dumb emotion, it's so incredibly beautiful. Sorrowful ballads with occasional falsetto passages. And even when I'm just listening to records I can see them moving on stage, doing the little whirls and gliding steps, flashing out their hands. Shiny bright hair. Custom tuxedos. Fantastic teeth and fingernails. And the cheap emotion behind the lyrics just wrecks me. The Motelles. The Vanities. The Willows. The Renditions. The Flairs. Nate Pearce and the Hydromatics. 'Baby can't you see how you're upsettin' me, shoo-eee, shoo-eee.' Everything is there, Bucky. There's nothing else I want or need."

"Where's Globke? Have any idea?"

"We haven't been in touch at all. Globke? Not at all."

"Where's Hanes?" I said.

"I never talk to Hanes. Globke's office boy? I never talk to him."

"I'm almost ready to make a move. But I need a certain item."

"Bucky, the people I front for are a business-oriented group. They know how to handle the item in question. They're not a bunch of knife-wielding dope fiends. They don't stockpile explosives. They're a force in the community. They're known on the street and they're known in the smoke-filled rooms and the corner offices."

"But are they known in the ladies' lounge? Are they known in the organ lofts and the prehistoric caves?"

"You said you're ready to make a move. Move into what?"

"The claustrophobia of vast spaces. Noise, echoes, noise. Not knowing which is which. People flaming out in the four-dollar seats."

"Are you afraid?"

"It's the only thing to do," I said. "Absolutely necessary to make the move. I'm betraying an idea I only half understand. But it's necessary. I'm betraying this room and these objects. But it has to be done. In that sense I'm afraid. I feel immense and heavy. I feel as though I'm being towed out of a hangar."

"There's nothing more frightening than the immensity and weight of blackness," Azarian said. "It's just so incredibly heavy. Getting into it is like sinking into tons of funky cement in order to arrive at some historical point where you can see who you are and who they are and how you've been historicized by the journey. Blackness has a hard firm smell all its own. It's like walking into a room in one of the Arab nations and all these guys in burnooses and sandals are standing around in the dimness and they're all smoking hashish and saying things you don't understand and everything smells of hash and unfamiliar feet and the tremendous intense weight of strange centuries. Centuries we never experienced. I don't know how I can make you feel the weight and heaviness. The smell that's both metallic and organic. The slowness of everything. The indifference of the black experience to the person who's trying to seek it out. It's the weightiest of all trips. I guarantee you. It's intense beyond belief. It's harder than the hardest drugs."

"The product isn't here. I don't know where it is. Happy Valley doesn't know where it is either. There's no business to be done."

"They'll give you first of all a bonus. Second a percentage. Third the option to invest. You get the bonus no matter how marketable the product turns out to be. They're putting pressure on me, Bucky. I'd like to resolve this thing."

When I woke up, Azarian was at the window looking out at the snow. I had no idea how long I'd slept. There were noises on the street, men unloading a truck. The woman leaned against the door frame, coat opened. I sat up in bed and stared at her, knowing it wasn't Azarian's security she was responsible for, nor mine. It seemed she was part of the pressure they were putting on him. Hair worn short. Caved face. Slender imperial neck. Hurdler's fused body. All in all a well-crafted piece of smoked glass and chrome. Azarian opened the window, scooped some snow off the ledge and tasted it.

"Needs seasoning," he said. "Want a bite?"

"Close the window."

"Epiphany used to sing in supper clubs, according to the data on her. Did I tell you that? Supper clubs. I didn't know places like that existed anymore. Must have been a weird scene. She acted in exploitation movies for six or seven months. A real pro-fessional. She did some modeling here and there. It's been a hard road. All that pro-fessionalism. It does things to people. Makes them hard."

"It don't faze Piffany," she said. "Nothing faze Piffany."

Azarian looked at her a while longer, then turned to me.

"So nobody knows where the product is."

"True."

"Including the people who were holding it."

"True again."

"I believe you, Bucky. You wouldn't mislead me in a situation like this. At least I can report back with a definite answer. No more skip-this and wait-on-that. I was tired of the whole thing. No more now."

"Are you afraid?" I said.

"Of everything. More than ever. Constantly."

Into boiling water I dropped the plastic pouch lumpy with beef chunks and frozen noodles. I watched it slide down the side of the pot as the water stilled for a moment before resuming its furor. There was no clock that worked, no way to measure the fourteen minutes deemed necessary for thawing and the regeneration of flavor. I counted to sixty a total of seven times, then multiplied by two and removed the pouch, cutting it open with a pair of rusty blunt grooming scissors found protruding from a beer can, one blade in each triangular incision. I waited for the long-dormant odor of goulash to be broadcast to my nose, smoke of herdsman's meat, but the air held little more than a limp whiff of carrots. I plopped contents into cornflake bowl and set to eating, eyes off the food, teeth working mechanically. I tried in fact to close off all my senses to this dim experience. Abused longhorns stuffed in pouches. Ceremonial flesh injected with cursed preservatives. Eating myself: lessons in the effects of auto-cannibalism. I tried to erase taste-memory from my lips with a two-ply paper towel, floral bordered. Then I got up and answered the telephone, chilled by the feel of the earpiece.

"It's your manager, who loves you. Don't ask where I

am. They tell me you've been on my trail, telephonically speaking. What I would call a sudden turn of events. You looking for me."

"Where are the tapes?"

"What tapes?"

"You had somebody go through this apartment. Transparanoia owns a key. I remember that. And I know you've got the tapes."

"What tapes?" he said. "I want to hear you say the whole thing. What tapes? Tell me in my ear."

"Mountain tapes."

"So those tapes. So those are the tapes you're referring to when you say I have the tapes."

"Where are they, Glob?"

"I don't have them."

"Of course you have them."

"Of course I have them. I've been thinking about those things every day for over a year now. Once you walked off the tour, I stopped thinking and started lusting. I got itchy fingered. I got wild. You walked off the goddamn tour, Bucky. You took away my action. We needed product, see. You were failing to deliver product. Product is something that matters deeply. You owed us product. Contracts in our files specified what product you owed, when it was due, how it was to be presented. This was not a question of a few thousand dollars gurgling down the drain. We're a parent corporation. We've got subsidiaries and affiliates all over the place. Do you know what they're constantly doing? They're yowling for their food. Feed me, feed me. Enormous sums of money were involved in your disappearing act. All these companies with their mouths opened wide for the worm breakfast, the worm lunch, the worm dinner. I needed the tapes to keep some kind of action going. Create demand for exotic product. Keep the public salivating. So I had a man hang around from time to time. Whenever you left the building he called me and I got down there quick-quick and snooped around hoping against hope to find the famous tapes. We also spent two days covering every inch of your mountain place. But I figured you were sitting on them. I figured they were right there in Opel's apartment. Trouble was you never left for very long. I couldn't give the place a professional Bogart-movie kind of going over. I entered on tiptoes and lifted up here and looked in there, dainty as a parakeet, covering my tracks before I even made any tracks. The night I finally got to the package was some terrific night because I don't know how many guys go charging up and down the stairs making animal sounds and stomping with their feet. Doors being smashed open and all kinds of commotion below me and then above me and there I am on tippytoes in the middle of the room with this package in my arms which I know contains the mountain tapes and this Mongol horde is racing up and down the stairs making sounds of conquest. I thought sure they'd break in on me and confiscate the object. When they left I heaved three long sighs and blessed myself in the Russian manner, right shoulder first, which my original wife used to do almost constantly before she got pissed off at God and started drinking vodka gimlets. Three sighs of relief. Thank you, Jesus, for letting me find the mountain tapes and for not letting those cuckoos come in here and butcher me, a poor senior executive performing his humble task."

"That's what amazes me," I said. "The fact that you'd

go to all that trouble. Your money, your position, your reputation. You more or less own this building, Globke."

"You don't understand, Bucky. You never carried obnoxiousness to its logical conclusion. Nothing is too personally distasteful for me to get involved in as long as it helps create a new product or extends the life of an existing product. Besides I don't want to get detached. Middle age and overweightness. These are enemies you can't fight from a swivel chair. Why do you think I don't have a chauffeur when my counterparts in the industry on both coasts have chauffeurs? I don't want to get detached. I want the challenge of traffic. I want to get down on my hands and knees and butt heads with the opposition. Action, action, action. It paid off, didn't it? I got the tapes, right? It was worth the trouble, wasn't it?"

"I was about ready to hand them over," I said. "I was ready to come back out."

"That pleases and delights me, Bucky. To think we're back in the old synchromesh pattern."

"I had to figure something out before I handed them over. I knew the tapes were a perfect answer in one sense. They were something unexpected, undreamed of, a whole new direction. But I can't go out before crowds and do those same songs. The effect of the tapes is that they're tapes. Done at a certain time under the weight of a certain emotion. Done on the spot and with many imperfections. This material can't be duplicated in a concert situation. So the tapes can be released, sure. But how do I get released? How do I get back out before crowds? I don't know how to work that little trick."

There was movement to my right and I looked quickly in that direction. Something white. Paper under the door. Neatly folded sheet. I told Globke to hold on and

I went to see who the latest bidder was for my time, influence and the objects in my possession. There was a brief message printed in tiny letters on the lined sheet. It took me a while to read it and put all the parts together. Bohack of Happy Valley. I went back to the phone.

"Somebody wants to see me. It concerns something I'd like to get out of the way. Let me call you back."

"You can't call me back. I'm unreachable. I'm with the tapes and I don't want to reveal any more of anything over the phone. I'm not giving out my number or my physical whereabouts. I'll be back at my desk tomorrow. We'll talk then. Don't worry about a thing. I not only know the answer to your question. I even know the question that follows the answer."

"Good. Very good. Terrific."

I went to the window as the message had specified. Three men crossed the street and came toward the building. I opened the door and waited. Two took positions against the wall behind the bathtub. The third was Bohack, an enormous man with a circular face and sparse beard. He leaned against the tub, smiling and slowly nodding. At a tangent to his easygoing manner was the barest trace of effort. The flesh near his eyes crinkled like rice paper and his lips were embalmed in that uninhabited smile of the world's more polite races. It seemed possible to abstract a fifteenth-century Chinese poet from the center of his face.

"Tremendous apologies," he said. "We never thought we'd have to infringe on Bucky Wunderlick like this. But here we are all the same. Goes to show you. This is Longboy and that's Maje. At the outset all we wanted to do was pay tribute to a man who separated himself from the legend of his legend and went into seclusion. But the tribute's gotten out of hand, causing x-amount of trouble. We came here to fill in the blanks because the sooner we do that the sooner we free Bucky Wunderlick from connection with the product. Do you know where Hanes is?"

"No."

"We can't locate Hanes. No trace of him. He's out there peddling. He's trying to make contact. It's a question of who gets where first. Do you know where Dr. Pepper is?"

"No," I said.

"First we couldn't locate Pepper. Then we got him and made arrangements. Now we can't locate him again. Do you know where Watney is?"

"No idea."

"We can't locate Watney to find out for sure if he was able to get his hands on the product. We know he was interested but we think he either failed to bid or his bid fell short. Okay — Azarian. Do you know where Azarian is?"

"No idea."

"We can't locate Azarian exactly. We know he was here and we know he flew to L.A. We figure he's gone back to the community group he's involved in that wants to rush new money into the ghetto and either rebuild from the ground up or destroy from the top down. But we can't locate him exactly. We don't know street name and house number."

"Does anybody know what the product is? I mean exactly."

"We won't know exactly until Pepper gets his mitts on it and goes into the lab."

"Who was it who went crashing through this building

one night? Breaking doors and stomping people. I mean exactly who was it? This one apartment wasn't touched. I think that means it was some kind of Happy Valley operation. But who exactly?"

"We've got a runaway contingent, Bucky. Their specialty is violence. Mindless violence. They talk about it all the time. When they're not talking about it, they're doing it. Mindless mindless violence. In a roundabout way that's what got them interested in wholesaling dope. Mindless violence is getting expensive. They need money to keep going."

"I wonder how they define mindless," I said.

"It defines itself. Mindless. In a way I can see what they're doing. Mindless violence is the only truly philosophical violence. They're scrupulous in avoiding any and all implications, political and otherwise. They have no real program or rationale beyond what I said. Mindless. I guess they're trying to empty everything out. Some of them have even taken new names. Bruno, Rex, Corky, Spot and King. They need money for mindless violence. We need money to maintain our privacy."

"You're all living together, is that right?"

"We're the Happy Valley Farm Commune," he said. "We still think that idea has a chance of working. We still talk to each other, group to group. We still live on the same floor of the same tenement. But now they've got two apartments and we've got two apartments and we're in the process of putting up barricades just to play it safe. We're not on bad terms with them. The rupture is a rupture in ideology. But since we're dealing with mindlessness we think it's a good idea to be extra mindful so we're putting up barricades in the hall between their quarters and our quarters. Privacy has its risks. Monkeys raised in isolation grow up violent."

"Rhesus monkeys," Maje said.

"Rhesus monkeys isolated at a certain phase of their development grow abnormally aggressive when that phase ends and they're exposed to other monkeys. They like to attack defenseless infant monkeys. Man the primate goes through similar phases. It may be that Happy Valley's life-style of privacy, isolation and so forth has spawned this outbreak of violence in half its members. Man the primate has been violent for only forty thousand years. What started it was abstract thought. When man started thinking abstractly he advanced from killing for food to killing for words and ideas. Maybe with mindless violence we're going into a new cycle. No more abstract thought and no more concrete thought. Violence for nothing."

"Nonviolence," I said.

"Personally I look on it as faggot violence," Bohack said. "Sexual connotation aside, something becomes faggot-laden when you remove all meaning from it. If there's one thing I learned in the six wasted months I spent in junior college being groomed to play football at USC, it's that violence without historical weight is basically faggot violence and basically ludicrous and a lot easier to ignore basically than the intense programmatic kind of violence that comes from having an idea to defend or some kind of historical impetus to support, like the idea of privacy or the impetus of privacy or the program of privacy. Rex and Spot and the others go flashing through buildings and careening off walls and shrieking at innocent victims and this demonstrates one of the possible results of the kind of intense inner-directed life we've been into, but not by any means the only result or the exclusive result. I played left tackle on defense until I realized my violence was faggot-laden."

"Laden with faggotry," Maje said.

I began to nod my head, trying to find a counterpoint to Bohack's nonstop bobbing. His slight diffident voice, never cresting, seemed to belong to an alternate entity, a small man lodged in his chest cavity, the square root of Bohack, a chap who wore shabby three-piece suits and combed his hair to one side. There was a sound in the darkness outside, rainfall, a sudden tumult over the city, strange, coming down like fury released, the passion of a summer's rain. Longboy scratched his straw head and then moused around in bulky pockets before coming up with a bent cigarette butt. He had the stale rangy look of someone who drives other people's cars coast to coast. He wore jump boots and a field jacket. Maje wore a lumber jacket identical to my own.

"What's in that airline bag?" Bohack said. "Just out of curiosity."

"Bubble gum cards."

"I'll tell you where we're located on the spectrum," he said. "Everybody misinterprets what Happy Valley is and where we're at. We get nothing but faulty interpretation on these subjects. First, what is Happy Valley? Happy Valley is the Happy Valley Farm Commune. We're defining ourselves as we go along. We're seeking our identity. That's why we came to the city. We came here to find ourselves. Second, where are we located on the spectrum? Okay, I have this to say. To heck with the environment. To heck with fresh vegetables. Heck with the third world. Heck with all idea of religion, God and the universe. We believe in the idea of returning the idea of privacy to the idea of American life. Man the primate has given way to man the mass transit vehicle. Mass man isn't free. Everybody knows that who's got one iota of common sense. Happy Valley is free. Free and getting freer. There's no land left. You can't go out West to find privacy. You need to build inward. That's the only direction left to build. We're building inward. We're hoping to wholesale dope to make the money to build inward. This isn't an easy concept to explain, understand or defend. But we believe you're the last person we have to defend ourselves to. We're your group-image, Bucky. You've come inside to stay. You've always been one step ahead of the times and this is the biggest step of all. Demythologizing yourself. Keeping covered. Putting up walls. Stripping off fantasy and legend. Reducing yourself to minimums. Your privacy and isolation are what give us the strength to be ourselves. We were willing victims of your sound. Now we're acolytes of your silence."

"What are your plans for Hanes?" I said.

"We'll find him," Maje said.

"Then they'll find him," Longboy said.

"Belly up in shit's creek," Maje said.

Longboy kept blowing on the gnarled butt to keep it lit. He never put it to his mouth to smoke. He merely whistled into its tip, forcing an occasional glow, man the primate making fire, a brown hem appearing on the paper as the heat bit in.

"Whose picture is on those bubble gum cards?" Bohack said.

"Watney's."

"Mind if we take a look? Just out of curiosity. Maje, go look."

"I see bubble gum cards."

"Whose picture on them?"

"Watney's," Maje said.

"Tear one card carefully apart, separating front from back."

"I don't know if they're thick enough to tear that way."

"Tear," Bohack said. "Pretend you're tearing apart an English muffin. Gently. Little by little."

"Here we go."

"What's in there?"

"Nothing."

"Take five more cards and tear them the same way. Front from back. English muffins. Easy now."

"What are you looking for?" I said.

"I'm not sure," Bohack said. "But Watney is Watney, a man with a reputation for being unpredictable. I'm sorry we've had to encroach on Bucky Wunderlick like this. But at least it's just about over now. We're on the verge of freeing Bucky Wunderlick from connection with the product and we won't have to encroach anymore."

Longboy licked the tip of the butt and returned it to his pocket. On his field jacket was an 82nd Airborne patch. Maje looked at Bohack.

"Take five more cards and tear them front from back," Bohack said. "Just five more. Just out of curiosity. A random sampling. Five more and then just five more. Front from back. Gently. English muffins."

20

"THE EFFECT of the tapes is that they're tapes."

"Sure, sure, sure. I agree. Absolutely. I'm with you. It's you and me. Absolutely. Teammates. Rah, rah, rah."

Globke was a toy motor in my ear, evidence of the muggy passion of telephones, his voice feverish with allegiance. He was largehearted in his sovereignty, dispensing benedictions to every quarter, a healer and teacher, prepared to animate what was moribund in me, to lash what was reluctant, to tease and feed the smallest fires of my mind.

"Talk, I'm listening. Tell me freely what's worrying that boy-genius head of yours. I'm sitting here with so many answers they're coming out of my clothes. Just make sure you don't ask me where I was with the tapes last night because I can only answer that in the flesh, person to person, and even then I'll have to whisper it in your ear just to make sure there's no security leak. I don't tolerate laxness in that area. My people know that. So do my people's people."

"How do I face crowds?" I said. "I can't do the material on the tapes. I don't want to do old material. I don't have new material. So how do I get back out? I don't know how I do that."

"You don't know how because it's not your appointed task to know how. It's not your professional identity. It's not your blood and muscle. But I know how, Bucky. I know exactly how."

"Okay."

"Guest appearances," he said. "We've got bands touring all over the country. You show up with one group in one place, a different group two nights later a thousand miles away. Surprise appearances. We don't announce anything to anybody. This way we build up tremendous interest. It's not only your return to action. It's not only a secret appearance. It's a whole series of appearances, different places, different times, weeks on end, never any clue where you'll show up, or when, or which group. Nobody knows, including the bands you appear with. You just show up, say hello and go on. We build up fantastic interest and suspense. Tremendous speculation on your movements and whereabouts. You're in Seattle one night, New Orleans the next. Crowds go wild wanting to know where you're going to turn up next. Every band you perform with is under contract to Transparanoia but that's the only clue anybody has and we've got enough bands blasting away out there to make it impossible for anybody to pinpoint your itinerary. We build up unbelievable publicity for the tapes. All these performances lead up to the release of the mountain tapes on a two-record set. By the time you're on the road, word will be out about the tapes. So all the time you're out there,

197

you're building up unprecedented interest in the tapes. You tour. Then we release the album. Then you tour again. I know what you're about to ask."

"What material do I perform?"

"You're about to ask what material you perform for all these concerts weeks on end with totally different groups. Bucky, it doesn't make the slightest bit of difference. You can jam, you can whistle, you can hum, you can do top-forty AM schlock, you can just stand there and shout at the audience. It doesn't make any difference what you do. The idea is to get you out there, get the whole mystique going again, make them wet their pants, make them yell and scream. Jam. That's what I say. Tap the mike and start picking. Do twenty minutes' guitar work and get the hell off. Make loud sounds, that's the thing. Move your lips, that's even better. Stand there and move your lips. Don't think of it as a performance. Think of it as an appearance. You're back on the road, that's the thing we're concerned about. Twenty minutes and run for the airport. You pick up one group in one city, zoom over to another city and another group, hit a third city and a third group, jump into a fourth city and pick up the original group there. We build up incredible interest this way."

"And the day after my funeral you release the tapes."

"You can't wait to get out there. Admit it, Bucky. You know the truth about the tour. You know you need the tour. It won't be long. Six or eight weeks, more or less. Then we release the material on the tapes. Then you hit the road for six or eight more weeks. A two-record set. Early spring release. Obvious title: *The Mountain Tapes*. We'd be crazy to call it anything else since that's the name everybody knows it by. Right now we're culling. We're editing down to twenty cuts. Getting rid of tape hiss and other noises. Snipping and clipping. Moving things around. Making up titles. Mixing in some instrumental work on about three quarters of the cuts. The thing's going to be rough as hell. But I think that's what we need right now. We've had enough of instant phasing and sixteen track and synthesizers. The people want something plain. Plain but complicated. The kind of material you and only you can deliver. I don't go in for levels in popular music and I don't even know if this is level-material or not. Maybe that's the power of it. Is it one level or two levels or no levels at all? Are the levels simple levels or profound levels? That's the power of the mountain tapes as I view it from my own particular viewpoint. It's not my sound. It's not the sound I listen to when I look across the river from my bedroom window on a summer night and my wife is sitting up in bed reading the Eastern teachers and there's moonlight on the river and the great rotting towers of Manhattan are arrayed across the night and I turn off the air conditioner and open a window and insert a cartridge in my music system. Your sound frankly isn't the sound I listen to at times like that. But it's a valid sound and it should sell by the carload. So right now we're culling and mixing and refining. The technical minds are hard at work. We aim for early spring. Definitely a two-record set. Positively called *The Mountain Tapes.*"

"First pressing of a hundred million billion," I said.

"I'm in the middle of arrangements for the tour. Everybody's working on it here. Late nights, weekends, quickie lunches. It'll be unprecedented, Bucky. Give me a few days to work out the second tour. Then we'll talk again. I've got tour one just about nailed down. Then we have to do some coordinating. Then we have to work out chart cities versus test cities. It's a valid sound. No doubt about it. I'll tell you where you'll be traveling the first time around. You want to hear? I've got the list right here marked confidential in big red letters."

"Not now," I said.

"The third, a Wednesday, Atlanta. Fourth, Memphis. Fifth, San Antonio. Sixth, Dallas. Seventh, New Orleans. Eighth, Albuquerque. Ninth, L.A. Tenth, Portland. Twelfth, Seattle. Thirteenth, Portland. Fourteenth, Tampa. Jacksonville the fifteenth. Miami the sixteenth, a Tuesday. Milwaukee the seventeenth. Flint the eighteenth. Grand Rapids the nineteenth. Grand Rapids the twentieth. Long Beach the twenty-first. Phoenix the twenty-second. Emporia twenty-third. Oneonta twenty-fifth. Cortland twenty-fifth. Brockton twenty-sixth. Toronto twenty-seventh. London twenty-eighth. Salt Lake City thirty-first. Lubbock the first, a Thursday. Houston on two. Galveston on three. Baton Rouge on four. Nashville on five. Memphis on six. Chattanooga on seven. Knoxville on eight. Alliance the tenth. Millersburg the eleventh. Ripley the twelfth. Bradford the thirteenth. Wellsboro the fourteenth. Hazelton the sixteenth. Woodland the seventeenth. Calistoga the eighteenth. Cloverdale the nineteenth. San Francisco the twentieth, a Tuesday, fog rolling in, sea gulls sitting on the pilings."

The Mountain Tapes

Press Preview and Record Industry Orientation
Edited transcript of lyrics—Tape 4

Prepared by Esme Taylor Associates
in collaboration with Pulse Redactor Co.

DIVISIONS OF TRANSPARANOIA

15:   Near and far
Night so high
Water falling
Water falling

Night so high
Water falling
Night so high
Water falling

Water falling
Water falling
Near and far
Water falling

Near and far
Night so high
Water falling
Water falling

16:   Dadmom sis
Driving in the black car
Dadmom sis
Sighting on the white line

Long come something
In a blinding light
Long gone something
In a blinding light

Dead all dead
Oooh all dead

Bloody foot
Bloody head

Eat the nose for Christmas
Eat the toes for Lent
Eat the car for Eat-A-Car
Send the bones to Kent

17:   Roses roses never red
Sweet the buzzard sings

Tell me tell me tell me
Time weather seasons
Story tell
Lesson give
Maiden words to learn

Being young restores the god
That eats itself
That eats itself
Better than the feast that ends
When they pick us from their teeth

Tell me tell me tell me
Cloud that's making
Less of sky
That more of flying
Tries to make

Down the wind it comes
Something flying down the wind

Time weather seasons
Maiden words to learn

Standing sitting
Strip by strip
I pick the skin from off my face
Becoming god
Begin to glow
Behead the rose

Better than the feast that ends
When they pick us from their teeth

Tell me tell me tell me
Roses roses never red
Soft the vulture croons

18:     I was born with all languages in my mouth

Baba
Baba
Baba

This and that
Egramine and woe
Sandwords on mud
High taljonics

Everything ever spoken shines from my teeth

Baba
Baba
Baba

Halda Ny Wadji
Hilda Krywicki
Mildred Hayes
Bionongenics

Mambo magic
Oh oh oh oh
Mambo madness
Oh oh oh oh

Dancing on a Latin balcony
Swaying to a starry symphony
Mambo mania
Oh oh oh oh

Undreamed grammars float in my spittle

Baba
Baba
Baba

Gadung gadung gadung
Uma childa nobo
Distiptics in wine
Insane today

I was born with all languages in my mouth

Baba
Baba
Baba

Nothing-maker
But to blurt

But to sing
Baby god and goo

19:   Nighttime come
      Mountain dark
      Treetop wind
      Mad dog bark

20:   I know my toes
      One to ten
      This one's big
      This one's no
      Big one big
      No one no
      I know my toes
      One to ten

      I touch my hand
      One touch one
      One is touching
      One is touched
      Touching touching
      Hand touch hand
      I touch my hand
      My hand touch me

      I smell my nose
      I smell my nose

I know my toes
I touch my hand
I smell my nose
I close my mouth

DO NOT QUOTE WITHOUT PERMISSION

21

IN A MILLENNIUM or two, a seeming paradox of our civilization will be best understood by those men versed in the methods of counter-archaeology. They will study us not by digging into the earth but by climbing vast dunes of industrial rubble and mutilated steel, seeking to reach the tops of our buildings. Here they'll chip lovingly at our spires, mansards, turrets, parapets, belfries, water tanks, flower pots, pigeon lofts and chimneys.

I turned south on Broadway.

Scaling our masonry they will identify the encrustations of twentieth-century art and culture, decade by decade, each layer simple enough to compare with the detritus at ground level — our shattered bank vaults, cash registers, safes, locks, electrified alarm systems and armored vehicles. Back in their universities in the earth, the counter-archaeologists will sort their reasons for our demise, citing as prominent the fact that we stored our beauty in the air, for birds of prey to see, while placing at eye level nothing more edifying than hardware, machinery and the implements of torture.

Hanes was sitting in the last car on the downtown local. The package angled out of an airline bag between his feet. I sat next to him, drawing a tap on the wrist. The noise was devastating, a series of bending downriver screams. Conversing I tilted my head and spoke directly into his ear. There were four or five other people in the car. Hanes looked weak and sick, a reproduction of my image in the mirror when I first arrived at Great Jones and cut myself shaving.

"What do you want?" I said.

"There's a rumor you're in New York living in an old building on some obscure street. Seriously, that's the strongest rumor about you right now. I've been to enough places lately to know which rumors are current and choice. I've been through so many time zones I'm almost bodiless."

"What places?"

"Literally or figuratively?" he said. "Literally about fifteen cities in three countries. Thought I had a sure sale at one point. Not quite, as it turned out. Question of ethics, they said. Time zones nearly did me in. I couldn't write my name on a traveler's check. I couldn't add simple figures. That was the literal journey I took. Figuratively I lived in a lamasery in Tibet, being guided through the mysteries of the highest level of death. That's what my whole vacation was about. Death-in-life. A string of make-believings. I moved through progressions of passive trains of thought. Nobody wanted to use me. I was prepared to be used. I did everything but take out ads in the newspapers. It was all a mistake. I'm meant to ride elevators floor to floor. More than that requires the mettle of demigods like yourself. I'm meant to crouch in stairwells reading inter-office mail. There's a tremendous lure to becoming bodiless. I see it but fear it. It's like a junkie's death. A junkie's death is beautiful because it's so effortless."

Hanes insisted on changing trains every few stops. We spent the afternoon this way, shouting into each other's head, standing on platforms, hurrying through barren tunnels, altering our level of descent from train to train. In the last car again, somewhere beneath the ruck of Red Hook, we saw a boy and two girls steal a sleeping derelict's shoes. The man stirred, then curled more tightly into the bouncing seat. Opening the door between cars, the three children headed for the heart of the train.

"Too young to understand the dignity of shoes," Hanes said.

"Why did you call me?"

"I keep moving. I haven't stopped since I got back Those people are not pleased with me. You'll have to intervene, Bucky. Return the product to Happy Valley with my deepest regrets for the delay involved. My vacation ends tomorrow morning. I'm due back at the office. Clearly I can't appear in such an obvious place with Bohack lathered up the way he undoubtedly is. What do I do then? I can't go to my apartment. I can't keep riding subways. I can't get on another plane and soar away. You'll have to intervene."

"No good," I said.

"You'll have to tell them you've got the product and it's theirs for the asking, no harm done, just show a little compassion toward Hanes, boys, he forgot himself and tried to turn dealer. His fatal taste for silver. But no harm done, right, boys?"

"You don't need me. Do it yourself. Just give it back and say you're sorry. I'm tired of that package. Don't want to see it anymore."

"My vacation ends tomorrow," he said.

We changed trains one more time. A woman wearing torn clothing and a surgical mask stood laced to one of the poles. About a dozen young students got on, dressed in black, nodding their bodies to the train's demonic flutter, serene rabbinical boys, hair solemnly curlicued, their ears like desert fruit. A man brought up battle sounds from his scarred throat. Creatures of the subway passed through the weaving cars. A woman across the aisle, carrying fifteen or twenty shopping bags inside each other, leaned forward and spoke to us.

"What happened to all the young men on shore leave from the air force? You never see them anymore. What's been done to them? There's something fishy going on. People know it in their bones but they won't say it out loud. Everybody's missing. Little by little everybody's disappearing. In our bones we know it."

We got off the train and walked through a series of cold passageways. Hanes carried the airline bag cradled to his chest. A strange wind lingered in the tunnels. The stone walls seemed to have a refrigerating effect and I submerged myself in my coat. Train-noise reverberated over our heads and beyond the blank walls. A small man stood in position before a monolithic hooded trash container, a neat stack of newspapers in his arms, waiting to be added to. I turned a corner and moved toward the stairway.

"You have to talk to them, Bucky. Make jokes. Tell them what a slimy child I am. Once they're off balance, move in with the old show-biz compassion."

"No good."

"The dignity of shoes," Hanes said. "The dignity of a record changer with a solid walnut base. The dignity of room equalizers. The dignity of a custom designed speaker component group."

I left him in the subway. There was still about an hour of light and it wasn't nearly as cold on the street as it had been below. A woman and two men looked closely at me, gesturing almost imperceptibly to each other as I walked past them. I stood across the street from the building on Great Jones, realizing I'd never before considered it as a total unit, having limited myself, in the visual idiom of the area, to the lower parts of small tenements, the middle and upper parts of the cast-iron titans. There wasn't much to see, no tilted skylight or skinny minaret, just Fenig hunching past his window. Beauty enough for the upward diggers. The poet's noble bones buried with his manuscripts.

After Hanes, events moved with virgin speed. The time was near when I'd have to return my body to the thermal regions and so I made minor raids on the night, a kind of training procedure, venturing out on circular journeys, extending the radius each succeeding time. Virgin speed. The thermal regions. Each succeeding time. The first event after Hanes was a phone call from California. Dodge. I hadn't talked to him since I'd left the tour in Houston and it took me several seconds to place the voice. Dodge played bass guitar in the last two groups I'd headed, a loose-limbed scrawl of a boy, never more at home than when having his stomach pumped. Our connection was excellent.

"Azarian's throat's been cut. They found him in the back of a gutted TV set that was sitting in a vacant lot in Watts."

"Strange," I said.

"It was a real big Magnavox console. He was stuffed into the back. Dead about ten hours when they found him. My mother's been trying to reach him all day."

"Strange. So strange."

"My mother's a spiritualist. I don't know if you knew that, Bucky. She's getting real good at it. But she thinks Azarian might be too far away. She can't establish voice contact. The vibrations are there. It's just that he's too far away to talk to."

"Weird," I said. "Oh so weird."

22

NEAR MIDNIGHT Menefee led me in the rain to a meeting with Dr. Pepper. He sheltered me with a large black umbrella, the kind doormen use, almost twice the normal size. Our route was circuitous in the extreme, full of loops, detours and backtrackings. A man emerged from beneath a freight platform and came toward us, barking strange words, his hair pasted straight back in choppy wet strokes, like a Cuban prize fighter's hair. He lunged at Menefee, who tossed the umbrella away and backed quickly to the middle of the street where he leaped repeatedly in panic, inundated by his own cape.

"New York!" he screamed at the man. "New York! New York! New York!"

The man, who'd stopped only long enough to lunge, continued on his way. I picked up the umbrella and tried to calm Menefee. We turned a corner, doubled back and then walked north on Lafayette. There was nobody in sight and the rain fell heavily. A car went by and Menefee lowered the umbrella until the spokes grazed our heads.

Water began to flood the sewers and when we crossed a street we had to wheel around the estuaries developing at every corner.

"Azarian's been murdered."

"Far out," he said.

On Astor Place he pointed to a city bus parked on the dark corner where the route begins and drivers take their break. The front door was open and I got on, leaving Menefee on the sidewalk. Dr. Pepper was sitting on the long seat at the back of the bus. I joined him there. He was hatless this time, dressed in a belted trench coat equipped with buttons, zippers, flaps, epaulets and at least four pockets. Although it was dark in the bus I could tell he was wearing perforated shoes.

"Driver's having a cup of coffee over at Iggy's. He's a good boy, friend of mine. I have friends in low places. I cultivate such people. It pays to have friends in low places. I find they do more for me in the long haul than the average maker and shaker."

"Azarian's been murdered," I said.

"He was a good boy," Pepper said. "Never met him myself. But the word on him was good. A good boy. I heard they did a number on his throat."

"That's what they did. Last time I saw him, he had a destroyer escort. Black woman. About twenty-five. Dressed for the heavyweight championship of the world. Epiphany Powell. I'd say she was five-eight, kind of dumb-sounding, no marks or scars."

"She's a police informer. Her name's Ferry or Sperry or something. Bureau of Narcotics Enforcement, et cetera, et cetera, state of California, so on, so forth."

"This is ending for me. I've got other things on my mind. What do you want to see me about?"

"Hanes," he said. "Hanes first and foremost. Has he tried to get in touch with you? Has he tried to lay off the package? These questions need answering, Buck."

"Hanes is riding the subways. If you want the package, go hunt him down."

"Your tone of voice doesn't go unnoted," Pepper said. "I guess if anybody's got the right to be irritated by all the amateurism on display, you and I would be the ones. This whole affair is beginning to rankle. Too much booshit being thrown around. I've maintained a high level of professionalism for a good many years and this dipsy-doodle stuff is affecting my equilibrium. I've set lofty standards for the whole damn profession. I could tell you about the Brownsville dope wars. Dave Grady and his microbus. The cocaine nun."

"Not right now," I said.

"Your tone is duly noted. Tell you why I asked you here, Buck. To get a fix on Hanes. See, we've got to wind this thing up. The dog-boys are running wild. Bohack is getting edgy. Azarian's black legions are poised. The narcs are everywhere. All in all the next few days figure to be crucial. If I can't get to Hanes in forty-eight hours, I'm pulling the hell out. This is a reluctant move but it's a move I've got to make for the sake of my own safety. Too many amateurs. Look what happened to Azarian, a good boy. Consider what may happen to Hanes, a homeless lad, orphan of the storm. It's definitely an unpromising future that boy appears to have. That's why I've got to liberate the product. Get it and fade. Leave Happy Valley to its own devices. Buck, you and I are the only parties in positions of mutual trust. Now I know you've been in touch with Hanes. All you have to do is point me in his direction. It's an act you'll never regret. Damn shame to see a dream product end up in the hands of unschooled people. Once-in-a-lifetime stuff. Do this thing, Buck. Point me toward Hanes."

"He's in the subways. That's all I know. He's got the product with him. I told him I wasn't interested in taking it off his hands. I've got other things. I told him to keep it."

"You amaze me, Buck. It's a street-wise gent you're talking to. An old politico of the back rooms. Do you realize what you're telling me? You're saying you came within arm's length of the product and you didn't make a grab. That story has no hair on it. I thought we were partners. I thought sure we'd be able to function in an atmosphere of mutual trust. Guess I'm losing my judgment. Getting all mellowed out. This grieves me, Buck. Dog-boys are running wild. U.S. Guv is sniffing at my laundry. I thought sure I had one ally in this whole sorry league of misfits. Hell of a note. Deeply disappointing. Face to face with Hanes. The product within arm's length. I assume that to be the case. Is arm's length an accurate term of measurement to the best of your recollection?"

"We shared a subway seat. We walked through tunnels together. At times our cuffs touched."

"And I'm to believe you didn't talk him off the product? I'm to believe you don't have possession of said product? If not possession of, then access to. I'm to believe you and Hanes didn't make a deal? I'm to believe all this? Oink-oink. That's all, folks."

"Sorry."

"Well now," he said. "You grant me no leeway, friend. None at all. I'm forced to bring pressure to bear. Not by choice. Not by inclination. It's a matter of balance and edge. Circumstances weigh against me. Old alliances have fallen on evil days. I'm left with no cards but the last nasty trump. According to my sources you're going back out on tour. I was apprised on that fact no more than two hours ago. So take the following proposal home and mull it over. It's simple, Buck. Either get the product to me or I make arrangements to extend your sabbatical. You won't leave that room is what I'm saying. That room will become your past, present and future. Four walls and a flush toilet. Don't doubt I can make such arrangements. It won't be easy, I grant you that. It'll take maneuvering of the riskiest kind. Arf-arf. I'll have to cut my drinking water with a splash of Wild Turkey. Oh, I'll have to be right on edge, spit-shined, cold as a witch's tit. Your decision to make. Forty-eight hours. A generous allowance by anyone's reckoning. I'll be in touch soon after. Get the product to me, Buck. For the sake of both our souls. I've got to have it, son. It's the making of a legend."

It was Menefee's duty to escort me back to Great Jones Street. It had stopped raining but he kept the umbrella close to our heads, bringing it down into my face every time a car passed. Our outing was less roundabout this time, a feint to the east, a shallow probe north, then straight down Lafayette past the warehouses. Two women with aerosol cans were spraying insect repellent into a heap of abandoned furniture. When they were finished, they dislodged the frame of an old sofa and dragged it off.

"He was wearing perforated shoes."

"I know," Menefee said. "I tried to talk him out of it, the rain and all, but I guess he thought perforated shoes were called for. He's had them twenty years, he said. The man's uncanny. He's a master of apparel, a master of vocal dynamics, a master of the odd fact. He's got style, he's got guile. Good thing he came along is all I can say in terms of my own development as a human thought module. I was being systematically depersonalized by the whole educational apparatus at the University of California at Santa Barbara and all I heard from my parents day after day in letters, phone calls and telegrams was that I should transfer to the University of California at Santa Cruz, which they wanted me to do for their own selfish grabby reasons, probably tinged with incest. So I got myself apprenticed to Dr. Pepper and since then I've developed unbelievably in terms of seeing myself as a full-service container with access outlets. So there we were traveling all around. So my parents said where are you? So I said I'm back in school. University of California at Pittsfield, Massachusetts."

Menefee closed the great umbrella and walked up the stairs with me. He checked the apartment before allowing me to enter. Then he left like a mythological bird returning to its jeweled nest. There was no heat. I ran the bath water and undressed. The water turned cold almost immediately but I let it run until the tub was nearly full. Then I took a bath, scrubbing my body with a hairbrush, outlasting the series of deep quakes that passed through me. When I stepped out finally, I was colder than the room.

23

"I HAVE a terminal fantasy," Fenig said. "It comes to me
more and more often, a recurring obsessive thing, and
I add little details every time. Funny how I never get tired
of this fantasy. I never get tired of it and I never feel the
need to purge myself of it. Here it is, word for word as it
comes to me, or as I come to it, whichever happens to be
the case. Listen and tell me what you think. Terminal
fantasy. I'm living all alone in this building. Outside the
dog-boys are pursuing their life-style of constant prowling.
They roam the empty streets, picking a building at random
and then crashing right in to execute their punches and
kicks, breaking down doors, charging up stairs, loping
through the hallways. I'm living here all alone. During
the day I write and think. I make tomato soup on my little
table stove. I spread butter on the saltines. I pour a glass of
Budweiser, the king of beers. This is my basic meal which
I have almost every day between my two basic sessions at
the typewriter, provided the juices are flowing. The heart
of the terminal fantasy is what happens at night. At night

I do some prowling of my own. I prowl this very building. With me, fore and aft, are two vicious German shepherds. I carry a pump-action shotgun snug against my belly. Floating at my right hip is a giant machete, lodged in a special customized cartridge belt. I go up and down the stairs virtually all night, me and the dogs. I look in every dark corner. I peer into the end of the darkest hallway. I check under the steps on the first floor. I conduct a thorough surveillance of your former apartment and Micklewhite's former apartment. All around me the buildings are being invaded and I'm just waiting for them to reach here, to come loping in with their gangly strides. All day I write fantastic terminal fiction. At night I prowl the building. Finally they come, eight of them, armed with tiny knives and little wooden clappers like castanets which they clap near the ears of their victims in a ritual of childish Zenlike spite. I don't panic in the slightest when I see them. This is what I've been waiting for all the while. Casually I pump out round after round. The shotgun is magical, never needs reloading, makes a throaty noise that comes out in slow motion. Booo-ooo-ooom. I set the dogs on them and follow on a two-count, wading in with the machete to slash and chop. The whole thing is like choreographed movie violence, lovely blood, happening so slowly, the dogs leaping at the dog-boys' throats, the gray blade slashing, the ripe red blood flowing everywhere, lovely, so slow, slower than milk being lapped from a mama's breast. But the blood and violence please me less than the simple fact that it's all so terminal. Stark days and nights. No one in the streets. Whole building to myself. Dogs and dog-boys. I defend one thing. I am here not to defend my land or my art. I am here to defend my privacy.

I slaughter whoever breaches the stillness of this building. Guard duty through the night. Feeding raw meat to my dogs. Dragging the dead and wounded down the stairs and placing them along the street at intervals of ten yards. Pouring gasoline. Lighting the bodies. Bonfires of the dead and dying. It's frankly a gorgeous sight. Tomato soup and fiction through the day. Guard duty all the night. Why are terminal events so pleasing, I wonder?"

Fenig was seated on the large trunk that contained his manuscripts. He bumped the heels of his sneakered feet in elusive tempo against the front of the trunk. His clothes, freshly laundered, were the same as those he'd worn every other time we'd talked. Perhaps he bought items in fours and fives. It seemed possible this was everything he owned, five sweat shirts, five pairs of chinos, five pairs of tennis sneakers. Fenig and I intersected at curious places beneath the solvable plane. This made things simple, I thought. It's always easier to live with similarities because they provide the shadings needed for concealment. Opposites tend eventually to corrode whatever democracy of feeling they made possible at the outset. In Fenig's closet were four more Fenigs, laced, hooded, neatly creased.

"I failed at pornography," he said, "because it put me in a position where I the writer was being manipulated by what I wrote. This is the essence of living in P-ville. It makes people easy to manipulate. It puts people on the level of things. I the writer was probably more aware of this than whoever the potential reader might be because I could feel the changes in me, the hardening of mechanisms, the subservience to lust-making and lust-awakening. You have to be half-mad to be a great pornographer and half-Swedish to expose yourself repeatedly to outright porn without losing a measure of whatever makes you human. Every pornographic work brings us closer to fascism. It reduces the human element. It encourages antlike response. I the writer suffered these things myself. As my child-characters whipped and raped each other around the clock, they began to fall apart in my fingers, and I myself slowly began to fragment. Pornography's limits and stereotypes worked against me from the very beginning and yet just beyond some last line or boundary I could imagine a new kind of P-ville full of characters who never even touch each other. But I'm not going anywhere near it. I'm not half-mad and I'm only one-eighth Swedish so obviously this is the wrong genre for me. The market wasn't very lucrative anyway. Fifteen hundred dollars for a novel-length manuscript. I told them it's not just pornography, it's children's pornography. They said a pussy's a pussy no matter who it's attached to. Genitals always take precedence. If it's a question of mixed categories and genitals play a prominent part in one of the categories, then that's the rate scale you're working with. Listen, I'm happy to be free of it. I can entertain my terminal fantasy with a clear conscience. It's not as though I'm a lust purveyor or incipient totalitarian of the world of letters. I have a fantasy that involves other people's blood being shed but this fantasy isn't part of the thread of my life. It isn't consistent with who I am and what I do. It's just an isolated aberration, much of it taking place in slow motion. If I was still involved in pornography for kids, then I'd be worried about a thread, a string, a consistency. But I'm free of that category and free of its miserable rate scale. Fi-nance, I get twelve and a half per cent after five thousand copies. Fi-nance is big time. The market's dying except for fi-nance. Daytime dramatic serials are still pretty healthy but I personally shun TV as much as possible. TV is deep space, thin air, no oxygen. There and gone, my words tickling the ears of the walking dead. I'm definitely sticking with financial literature. Fi-nance is solid. There'll always be millionaires and people who want to be millionaires. I'm midwifing this thing very carefully. This is the watershed of my career. Let's face it, I've been turning out a pretty uneven oeuvre. I need a permanent base to express myself from. No more movement or fluctuation. I need to see a long line stretching straight ahead into the distance. The market's spinning slower and slower and the lights are dimming and all the loud sounds are dying out. The great wheel is running down, no doubt about it, but I surprise myself by being philosophical. Even if the financial market dies out with the rest of the market, I maintain a certain fragile hope for my own eventual redemption as a functioning writer. I see empty streets. I see a dead market. I see the dog-boys prowling. There I am at the typewriter. I'm old but still fit. My mind is clearer than ever. I'm at the height of my powers. I'm in firm control of my material. I'm writing terminal fiction and I'm writing not for the market, not for the quick sale, not for the sake of professionalism or my name in print. I'm writing for the survivors, that they may know what it was they survived. I'm writing, if you will, for posterity, that people may understand what went wrong and resist the historical imperative of judging us too harshly. I see tomato soup and saltines."

After a while he lowered himself from the trunk and made coffee. We drank it quietly. Fenig held the large cup with both hands. To drink he lowered his head to the rim, making a small sacrament of the act. It was roughly the middle of the day. I could hear my phone ringing for the third time in the past hour. Fenig poured more coffee. He took his cup to the typewriter table this time. Soon he began to scratch at the keys, first with two fingers, then with his left hand, thumb capering on the space bar, eventually both hands working, ten fingers crashing on the keys, his head moving closer to the black machine, eyes appearing to follow the arc of each metal slingshot hurling ink upon the page.

I went downstairs and fell asleep almost immediately. The telephone rang and I dragged myself over there to lift away the noise. It was Watney somewhere in the British Isles.

"Back finally?"

"Here I am," I said.

"Rang up before, Bucky. Three times exactly. No answer. Odd, I thought. Man's not there. Wonder where, I thought. Wonder where the central figure in this rapidly evolving scenario is off to. Odd, innit? That's what I thought."

"I'm back finally."

"Bucky, I'm contacting you as per our conversation of the twentieth last."

"What conversation?" I said.

"We agreed I'd ring you at a specific time, such and such a day. That's what I've been engaged in for the past hour. In other words I'm carrying out the specifics of our joint proposal as agreed upon. You said then you had no compass bearing on the product. I officially ask if the time is now a bit more propitious for a serious bid on the part of my Anglo-European associates and myself, as far as astrology and the gods are concerned."

"The product is out of my hands completely. I don't have it and I don't know how to get it. Somebody named Hanes has it. Five feet seven. A hundred and thirty pounds. No marks or scars."

"Somebody named Hanes," he said.

"That's right."

"Young. Slender. Fragile. Bored, sort of."

"That's him."

"Alabaster skin."

"That's him," I said. "Very descriptive. I like that. Oh, superb. Too bad he doesn't have an aquiline nose. You'd have a good combination going. But sure, that's him, that fits."

"He's had possession for a lengthy period of time, has he?"

"In terms of days or weeks I don't recall. But I know he's had the product since before you were here."

"Fancy, fancy," Watney said. "Seems I met Hanes in Toronto. He'd been lurking about for days. Dogging my every footstep. He came looking for me with that tarnished angelic look of his. Selling he was. What he called the ultimate drug. Selling outright. Selling shares. Selling European rights. He was flexible he was. See, all my information pointed to you, Bucky. You were the one with possession. I made my way through all of Canada, doing little bits of business here and there, laying groundwork, opening vistas. All the while intending to sneak up on the infamous Bucky Wunderlick and do some fanatical New York promoting. Lay a heavy-handed bid on my old comrade in arms. This boy Hanes came sauntering in with that desperate precious saunter of his. I gave it little thought I did. See, all the rumors in my dossier of rumors located the ultimate drug in your own notorious hands."

"Hanes ran off with it. He was supposed to deliver it somewhere and then negotiate a deal. But he ran off to deal on his own."

"Cheeky little bastard."

"You threw him out, I take it."

"Not a bit of it," Watney said. "I never toss people out the door. People are human beings. They're creatures of infinite capacity. They have immortal souls they do. No, I followed the usual procedure and sent a small sample of his wares by courier back to ground zero for analysis. Back to our clandestine waterfront laboratory somewhere in the center of Birmingham. Back to our first-rate technical lads in their white smocks and high-heeled shoes. I speak in riddles, of course. I reveal only the salient findings."

"Which were?"

"Let's see then. A volunteer took a poke in the arm. Since then all he does is dribble and whine. Our technical lads did their clever tests at first. But the results were vague. So they called a volunteer out of the line and gave him a poke. Our biggest problem comes from volunteers queuing up on the sidewalk in broad daylight. So bloody eager they are to serve the cause of science. Let's see then. The drug attacks a particular region in the left hemisphere of the brain. That's the verbal hemisphere, it seems. Where the words are kept. The boy's been reduced to chronic dribbling. Naturally when I got the report I informed your Hanes person that we wanted no part of his vicious product. Christ, ethics do exist. I told the technical lads they should have used a bloody cat. They pointed to the fact that cats don't speak in the first place. Thus small value in injecting a cat. Little did I know when sweeping into your flat with my accustomed grandiosity that I'd already had my hands on the much-sought-after product."

"Do you know where you left the bubble gum cards?" I said.

"The airline bag, is it? Is that where my man left it? Did he leave it with you? Blessy's truly dim, you know. It's not just a game we play. He wants watching, that one does. I shall have to rake him over the electric coals for this. Shall have to instruct that boy in the wages of sin. He claimed the driver of the limousine drove off with it. No harm done. But sets a nasty precedent."

"If it's not an unfair question, why do you travel around with bubble gum cards?"

"Not a bad likeness of me, is it? Taken some years back. All done up in blue velvet I was. A childhood dream come true. My own bubble gum card. They're magic cards, Bucky. Very hush-hush. Promise not to breathe a word."

"Okay."

"Truly promise. Put heart and soul into it. A soldier's oath. The vow of a pristine nun. Second thought, not much sense of obligation left in those quarters anymore. Give me a blacker oath. The kind they take in shabby inner offices. Narcotics agent. Postal inspector. Customs official. Give me an oath with blood on it."

"Brothers," I said.

"I take hundreds of bubble gum cards everywhere I go. The Watney bubble gum card. Hard-to-get item. Rarer than a pair of blue suede shoes in Tierra del Fuego. I've virtually cornered the market, you see. I've established a virtual monopoly. Sometimes two or three of the cards in my luggage are different from all the rest. These are the magic cards, a direct offspring of our own Industrial Revolution. Buy British, I always say. The magic cards are constructed in such a way that they can be sealed and resealed a number of times with our own private sealing agent. The tiniest sample of this or that item can be placed inside a miniature casing of anodized metal, which in turn is fitted into a given card and taken to a given place. Card unsealed. Item tested. We carried samples of microdot LSD in from Malta with Watney bubble gum cards. Thoroughly enjoy carrying the things about. Wonderful at parties. One's own bubble gum card. Good fun to flash on unsuspecting fellow passengers aboard a great jetliner streaking across the heavens. I enplane at point A. I deplane at point B. Blowing metaphorical bubbles all the way. Just ordinary cards in the bag Blessy left at your flat. None of the magics there. The magics were in the luggage proper. The heavy luggage. The real thing. The baggage. Sets a bad precedent however. Shall have to get grim with that boy."

"I'm going back out on tour. What do you think? Do you think I'm crazy? I feel I have to do it. Time's up. Have to make the move."

"Back out, is it? Back into the pits and dung troughs. Best provide for all contingencies, old Bucky. Prepare an overdose for the critical minutes. Have it sitting on the dresser. Ancient bitch of the road. Best do it, old friend. You don't want to drop apart gradually. Bad for the image. You're required to go all at once. Excess. That's the number under your name. I could never match the genius of your excess. I was too artificial. Had to make it all up and shake it all down. That was my critical failing. I failed to embody true and honest excess. I was just a wad of chewing gum on your shoe. So stick to the image, old Bucky. Prepare a careful OD and flame yourself away. Be deliberate about it. Be as thorough as humanly possible. Don't forget to lick the spoon."

"I want to become a dream," I said. "I'm tired of my body. I want to be a dream, their dream. I want to flow right through them."

"You have to die first."

"I knew I'd left something out."

"You have to die all at once. None of this gradual wasting away of the middle classes. You have to burst into flame. It's all a worthless gesture, of course. Sorry to be the one who has to bear this depressing message. But true, it's all worthless. One's death must be equal to one's power. The OD or assassination is esthetically lovely but in point of fact means little unless it reverberates to the sound of power. The powerful man who achieves a gorgeous death automatically becomes a national hero and saint of all churches. No power, the thing falls flat. Bucky, you have no power. You have the illusion of power. I know this firsthand. I learned this in lesson after lesson and city after city. Nothing truly moves to your sound. Nothing is shaken or bent. You're a bloody artist you are. Less than four ounces on the meat scale. You're soft, not hard. You're above ground, not under. The true underground is the place where power flows. That's the best-kept secret of our time. You're not the underground. Your people aren't underground people.

The presidents and prime ministers are the ones who make the underground deals and speak the true underground idiom. The corporations. The military. The banks. This is the underground network. This is where it happens. Power flows under the surface, far beneath the level you and I live on. This is where the laws are broken, way down under, far beneath the speed freaks and cutters of smack. You're not insulated or unaccountable the way a corporate force is. Your audience is not the relevant audience. It doesn't make anything. It doesn't sell to others. Your life consumes itself. Chomp. I hear it across three thousand miles of gray ocean. Chomp, chomp. I know illusions I do. Illusions forced me to change my life. I remember the end of my last regular tour in the music business. Broken man I was. Victim of illusion. No sorrier figure in all the realm. Shall I tell you how I tried to cope? Where I went and how I got there? It's a sad tale, it is. Promise you won't breathe a word. Have I got your oath in blood?"

"Sure," I said.

"Promised like a true friend. Truly promised. Shall I tell you then? Shall I tell you what I did?"

"Sure."

"I took a walk down Lonely Street to Heartbreak Hotel."

24

HER NAME came back to me the moment before he spoke it. He opened a bottle of warm champagne and we gathered together, at angles of caricatured intimacy, huddled all throo in the room's lone dollop of sunlight. Globke passed out the drinks in paper cups he had brought along, suspecting unsanitary conditions in the native glassware. Seated in my bowl-shaped chair, knees above my belly, I drank to the health of the mountain tapes.

"Bucky, you remember Michelle."

"Definitely."

"You had dinner with us over at our place about a year ago, right after we just moved in."

"I remember."

"We had roast leg of lamb and two kinds of wine. Michelle made those fantastic Hindu vegetable things she makes. We listened to highlights from *Madame Butterfly*. We sipped our wine in the candlelight."

"I remember," I said.

"Then we sat on the upper terrace and talked about the

uses of money. Then we talked about greed. Then we talked about the misuses of money. Then we had tea and that gummy dessert-shit I hate so much. Then I called a limousine to take you to the airport. So anyway here she is. My young wife. Wife, mother, lover, colleague, friend. You remember Michelle."

"Sure," I said.

"Don't touch her," Globke said.

"I won't."

"It makes me nervous when she gets touched. See, oldness and fatness. See that? See what it does? Makes me a figure of fun. But I'm not succumbing without a fight. I'm pushing on ahead. I'm double-clutching through middle age. You should have seen me when I got my hands on the tapes. I was all action. My voice crackled with authority. I rounded up personnel, made plans, gave instructions. Then I put the tapes in my Pan Am flight bag and flew off in the night to Cincinnati, where I called you from. Combination studio–warehouse– record plant. Small but big enough. Known to few. A place where for years they recorded marching bands and high school chorales. Cincinnati. Queen city of the early West. All technical work on the tapes plus final pressing being done there. Call it unfounded fear but I was afraid to take that material anywhere else. Too much chance of sabotage. Material that there's no way to duplicate can't be handled like a job-lot product. We drink to the mountain tapes. The mountain tapes. Keep them safe, God of my fathers, until the record's in the racks."

"When do I leave?"

"We drink to the tour now. The tour. Day after to-morrow, Bucky. Zap, you're gone. Drink up, everybody.

It's all set. Day after tomorrow. We inaugurate the greatest record promotion in history. In fact I'm leaking word about the mountain tapes starting today. Tomorrow I begin co-opting the rumors behind the reason for your comeback. You've got an incurable disease. One year to live. You want to spend it with your fans."

"Other rumors are bound to arise."

"Will they compare?"

"I guess not," I said.

"For sheer bad taste, will they compare? Will they even come close? I appropriate all other potential rumors. I sponge them up. They belong to me by divine right of bad taste. I come out of a tradition, Bucky. I'm not new money, new culture, new consciousness. I emerge from a distinct tradition. Bad taste. Michelle softens the edges of it but nothing can kill it completely. It's there to stay and I'm proud and delighted. The dynamics of bad taste is something they should investigate with a research grant. A fantastic subject. My whole life is a study in bad taste. Bad taste is the foundation for every success I've ever had. I'm a self-made mogul in an industry that abounds in bad taste. Look at me. Mogul is written all over me. How did I get there? Aggressiveness got me there. Massive double-dealing. Loudmouthedness. Insults beyond belief. Little white lies. Farts and belches. Betraying a friend and then bragging about it. These are the things that give you stature in the industry. Not just respect or clout or notability. *Stature.* It's not enough to betray a friend. That gives you respect at the very most. You have to supply the extra touch. You betray a friend and then you brag about it. That's star quality. That gives you stature. Do you know what I have on top of bad taste?

I have self-starting entrepreneurial instincts. The combination is unbeatable."

"I like your suit," I said.

"Chemical-stretch three-piece herringbone. Factory outlet. Clifton, New Jersey. Twenty per cent less than wholesale."

"Quietly assertive."

"I sold the movie rights for two hundred thousand."

"To your suit?"

"It goes before the cameras in late summer."

"You're in a good mood," I said.

"Do you know what this suit has that other suits don't have? Want me to tell you?"

"Go ahead."

"Star quality," he said. "This suit has star quality."

"You're really happy, aren't you? You're all puffed up with it. Action. You can't wait to send me off."

"But this isn't my favorite suit. Far from it. My favorite suit is the suit I bought at Simon Ackerman in the Bronx in nineteen hundred and fifty-four. Revolving credit was just starting then. And I'll tell you a funny thing if you want to hear a funny thing. That suit didn't fit me then but it fits me now. That suit did not fit me in nineteen fifty-four. You should see it now. But what they should do, they should date suits the way they date automobiles or fine wines. You could say I got a nineteen fifty-four Simon Ackerman. Shoulder fins and fully pleated. I got a nineteen sixty-eight Klein's basement. Forty-four dollars, wear it off the rack, turns purple when it rains. But you should see that suit now. Tell him, Michelle. Is it a fit or isn't it? Am I exaggerating or not? Are we here or aren't we?"

"Seen Hanes lately?" I said.

"Hanes is back at work. Hanes? He's back at work. Why do you ask, Bucky?"

"No reason."

"We power our way up the charts," Globke said. "We reach the break-even point. We determine our allocations. We gross and outgross. We work out test cities versus chart cities. We refill the record racks. We confer with our senior people. We climb and grab. We yell over the telephone. We sell and outsell. We display perpetual bad taste."

"The epics teach us that all work is equal to all other work," Michelle said. "Once we have freed ourselves of fear and desire, no act we perform is more important than the act that precedes it or the act that follows. Non-attachment is the path to beyond-reality. Beyond-reality is where our true nature indwells. The body is an illusion The epics teach us that men cannot leap across time to the eye of the absolute. Men must proceed in stages across many boundaries. Free of fear and desire, we find our true nature. Good. Goodness. God. Godhead. Evil is nothing more than attachment. Evil is attachment."

"Evil is movement toward void," I said.

"One and the same," she said.

Before they departed she came to my chair and put her lips to my left temple. She had the kind of face that allows love or pain to rise immediately to the surface, unshrouded face usually belonging to older women, those who've forgotten what must be shielded and what disclosed. What now she revealed was not a longing for me but rather a need for what she took to be my suffering. In her eyes and warm lips was the wish to be burdened, to take whatever I could not bear. Globke waited at the door, oddly deferential to the moment's solemnity. He held the empty champagne bottle under his arm, a souvenir (he'd said) of the day of my second birth.

That evening I sat by the window, imagining tiny men in black booties scampering out of the firehouse, the house itself on fire, flames leaping and smoke pouring, the little men skipping about in glee, men in booties and stunted red helmets, men with bushy eyebrows, tiny men all in a circle holding hands.

25

IN ABUNDANT SUNLIGHT a man carried paintings from a battered panel truck into the loft building across the street from me. He took canvas after canvas, about a dozen, gray every one with a white line down the middle. I turned back to Bohack, who occupied the center of the room, nodding into his Chinese beard, one foot up on a chair, the rest of him collapsing toward that point of support. He wasn't happy with me. His body showed it, swollen with exhaustion. He knew I was no longer content to remain in this room, leading his band of janissaries progressively inward, conceding motion to each hour that passed. His large open face seemed to beam his disappointment across the room. We were ten minutes into our second silence. Bohack took out a handkerchief and delivered mucoidal noises into it. He remained in his standing crouch, right foot set on the edge of the chair, elbow resting on right knee, his diffuse beard concealed by the handkerchief. He wasn't at all happy with me. I had betrayed our convergent destinies, reading the leer in the silvery eye of the first child to beckon.

"I wondered if you'd get here in time," I said. "I'm due to leave in a matter of hours. They're sending a car for me."

"If you knew I was coming over, why didn't you leave ahead of schedule? Why didn't Bucky Wunderlick get out when he had the chance?"

"Dumb question," I said.

"I guess it is. Heck, I'm stupid sometimes. You half want this confrontation. You half want to go to Essex Street with me."

"Who cut Azarian's throat? Did his people do that?"

"Longboy."

"What for?"

"Longboy's our throat man. When he was a medic in the Airborne he performed many a tracheotomy out in the field. Man with broken jaw, blocked air passage, choking to death in the drop zone. Longboy would trake him right there. He traked maybe ten people all told. He got to know the throat. He's developed a feel for it. So we sent Longboy after Azarian's throat. We had a lot of trouble locating Azarian. We knew he was after the product but we couldn't get him located right."

"He was just bidding," I said. "He never had his hands on it. There was no point in killing him."

"We killed him because we found him," Bohack said. "It was a heck of a job. We put a lot of time and effort into it. After all that time and effort, we obviously had to kill him. If we didn't kill him, it would have been a total waste, all that time and effort. We knew he was in California, in L.A., most likely in Watts. Finally we got street name and house number. That's when we sent out Longboy. He's our throat man."

240

"Dr. Pepper told you I was leaving. Is that right?"

"Right, Pepper told us. Pepper wanted me to arrange a get-together with Rex, Brandy, King, Bruno and the others. He knew about Happy Valley's interest in your retirement and he wanted to use the dog-boys to keep you permanently in this room. He was scared half to death of even approaching the dog-boys but he thought you'd cut him out of any chance at the product and this was his way of getting revenge. I was surprised, tell you the truth. I didn't think Pepper was that vindictive. He came on like a spiteful kid who wakes up one morning and finds he has two poison fangs and it's just a question of who gets the first nip. But I could tell he expected heap big trouble if he got anywhere near the dog-boys. Fear and trembling. It might have been halfway funny to see Pepper with those lunatics but I finally told him it wasn't necessary. I told him we didn't need the dog boys. Don't you want to know why? You're just standing there without any look on your face. Isn't Bucky interested? Doesn't he care about these things?"

"He cares deeply."

"The dog-boys aren't an independent pack. I control them. I run them back and forth. They're not a separate faction. They're just a lunatic fringe that we use for our own purposes. They're completely subordinate. There's only one Happy Valley Farm Commune. The dog-boys are the lunatic fringe. We use them to sow fear and confusion. People think Happy Valley's weak and disorganized when it's just the opposite. A nice touch, what do you think? Broadcasting dissension, what do you think? Not bad, right? Sowing fear. Sowing confusion. What's your opinion?"

"I need time to think about it."

"I gave them the names," he said. "Bruno, Rex, Corky and so on. What do you think? Nice touch, don't you think? Sense of humor. You need that."

"How heavy are you?"

"I go two forty-five. Is that too heavy? I've got a big frame. With a big frame you need considerable poundage. My face is a round-type face but the rest of me is packed pretty solid."

"Are your parents big people?" I said.

"They're both normal size except my mother has the biggest thumbs I've ever seen in my life."

"Any brothers or sisters?"

"Only child."

"Where do you buy your clothes?"

"Orchard Street."

"Do you pay your rent with cash, check or money order?"

"Right now we owe four months."

"What are your plans for me?"

"It's a nice day," he said. "Let's go up to the roof."

We strolled among chimneys of various shapes and materials, crumbling brickwork, heavy metal painted black, aluminum peanut-whistles. The tar was hard. To north and south, towers grew out of crooked rooftops in the foreground. Bohack rested against the ledge, eyes closed and face thrust upward, although the sun was at his back. It was one of those electrically blue days when every tall building set against the sky seems to drip silver. Bohack was looking at me now. His arms were folded. He wore crushed dented clothing that made him appear to ripple upward, a fountain of automobile parts and bland expressions.

"Your suicide should take place in a city like Tangier or Port-au-Prince or Auckland, New Zealand. Some semi-mysterious or remote place is probably best for your kind of suicide. That way the news is late, the news is garbled, the news is full of contradictions. A doubt always lingers that way. Even when they produce your body, there's a doubt or a shadow of a doubt. Maybe it's somebody else. Maybe it's a look-alike provided by the local police. The perfect suicide is when people know you're dead on one level but refuse to accept it on a deeper level. It's the final inward plunge, Bucky. It's what you owe us. It really is. We patterned our whole lives after your example. What happens? You decide to pull out. Just like that. You decide to step back into the legend. No good, Bucky. Not acceptable. Obviously it leaves us hanging. We're in the midst of an inward plunge and you suddenly just like that decide to sneak out into the open. Zero acceptability. Suicide's the best answer all around. I think you see that now."

"It's a good answer. But not the best."

"There's a definite second-best. But suicide's the best. How can I tempt you further? Can I say it's what everybody ultimately expects of you, right down to the littlest scribbler of fan mail? Should I say it's a life-affirming gesture for someone in your position? Do I put the whole thing in perspective by arguing that your life and work will draw off additional meaning from an act of this kind? How can I tempt you, Bucky? We're how high up — four stories? Not enough, is it? You want to be sure and I don't blame you one bit. Istanbul, that would be ideal. Better than Auckland, New Zealand, where chances are they do things in a neat tidy manner and we wouldn't have the proper mystery or doubt. Our building on Essex

Street is five stories high. Add one for the roof. That's six, which is probably high enough."

"I admit I'm tempted."

"It's by far the best answer."

"Not by jumping though. That's no good at all."

"Let's discuss alternatives," he said.

"Many better methods."

"I'd be happy to discuss them with you. Anything you have to offer in the way of ideas is great with me. Gun's not bad. It's a right-there kind of thing. It's got a brutal purity other methods don't have."

"You're not being serious," I said. "If you were really bearing down on this, you wouldn't make dumb suggestions. It has to be more passive. But not drugs and not gas. An exotic poison maybe. A snake in a basket. Something that harks back to the great days when excess was the style. But I'll tell you the truth, Bo. We're just making noises up here. I have no real intentions. I'm not innocent enough for suicide."

"You have to teach by example, Bucky. Otherwise you're just a salesman."

"I've done things without understanding them fully. This would be one more such thing. Besides I'm not innocent. I've ass-licked around the edges of some mean conceits. You can't kill yourself when you're half-rotten with plague. Only the innocent are received. No suicide gets through unless he's free of attachment. It's murder I've been burning to commit. I'm way beyond suicide."

"Who you plan to kill?"

"I guess nobody anymore. Not even in the vague way I meant it. Four ounces on the meat scale. That's all I'm told I weigh. I was thinking about that while I waited for you to get here. Whether to bother at all with limousines and planes or just take what Bohack's got in store."

"Second-best," he said. "There's a definite second-best."

He put his hands flat against his belly and slid them into his pants up to the knuckles. Under his jacket, opened to the mild afternoon, he wore broad red suspenders. We passed a yawn between us. To the east a drilling crew was blasting rock apart at a construction site. I heard but could not see them. Each blast was preceded by the sound of whistles and followed by pigeons angling in panic to other abutments.

"You found Azarian," I said. "You found Pepper or he found you. You didn't find Watney. Did you find Hanes?"

"Hanes found us."

"That's what I thought."

"The kid finally got around to using his God-given intellect. He offered to do anything we wanted if we'd give him a guarantee for his safety. He couldn't have called at a better time. There was one important service nobody else was in a position to render for us. Hanes was the right man at the right time. I look at your face and see nothing. Isn't Bucky Wunderlick curious about these things? Doesn't he care how the machinery functions? Maybe it's just that the sun's in his eyes. He seems to be blank but it's only the sun."

"I thought I had you measured step by step," I said. "I even awarded myself one extra step. But I have to admit I don't know what service Hanes might be in a position to render Happy Valley. The sun's in my eyes. Otherwise you'd see curiosity lighting up my face."

"We want your silence. You know that. But even if you took your own life right now, we wouldn't have what

245

we want. Why? Because of the mountain tapes. Because the tapes are about to be released. New legends, new sounds, new confusions. In the last few days there have been rumors about the tapes being released. Then Pepper told us you were going on tour. It all fitted together. The only thing we didn't know was how to get at the tapes. Where they were. Who had them. Silence is silence, Bucky. There's no silence with the tapes on the market. It would hurt us. It would cause psychological pain. So Hanes was the right man. We gave him the guarantee he wanted. In return he went through the confidential files at Transparanoia. According to him, it was easy. He had the answer in no time."

"Pittsburgh."

"Cincinnati."

"Just testing," I said.

"Hanes seemed eager to give you maximum knifage. To put the blade in six inches, withdraw it two inches, stick it in three more inches. Seven inches. Maximum knifage among the primitive blood cults."

"I didn't help him when he was in the subways."

"He remembered."

"I see that."

"So Maje and two others are in a car right now on their way to the record plant in Cincinnati. They're carrying about twenty pounds of C-four. We have to play it safe. We don't know what stage of production the record's at. So we're blowing the whole plant. Silence has to be total if it's to be called silence. Am I right or not? In order to earn the name silence, the silence has to be total. I'd like to hear your views on that."

I took eight steps forward and hit him in the stomach,

directing the blow at a point equidistant from his thumbs, which were still set against his belly, the only fingers outside his pants, about six inches apart, parallel to his belt line. I walked back to my spot at the brick chimney.

"What was that?" he said.

"Animal urge."

"What for?"

"I know what's ahead. Some dumb instinct made me hit you. No reason though. I walk step for step with you, Bo. It was an animal thing. I know what's ahead. I agree to it. But this animal urge made me hit you anyway."

"You get the faggot violence going. That's the only thing you accomplish with a move like that. The old faggot violence comes raging out of me. I turn bleary. I strike at anything that breathes. That's the meaningless inner faggotry everyone possesses. You roused my faggot-laden soul. Bad stuff, Bucky. No should do. Make nice-nice. No hit people. Heap big trouble."

"I agree to everything."

"It's a nice day," he said. "Let's go for a walk."

We went south on the Bowery without a word. Gray cats slept in the sun among men thawing against the sides of buildings, seated there for a parade of visored riot cops and their whores in snowshoes, or asleep as if in baskets, their bodies shaped against the revolt of bone. I had a yawning seizure then. It was fear, I knew, that caused it — the mechanism in the body that covers up fear in this whimsical way, yawn after yawn. The seizure lasted all the way to the Salvation Army Memorial Hotel, accompanied by popping sounds in my cheekbones. I was suddenly hungry. We stopped at a frankfurter cart on Chrystie Street and I ate three chili dogs and drank Coke

247

and orange soda. I felt sick and tossed the empty Coke bottle over my shoulder, hearing it break politely in the gutter. Bohack never spoke or touched me. People seemed to know him here, although no words were exchanged. We went east into the market streets. I vomited on a parked car. Bohack waited at the distance deemed correct in the etiquette of vomiting. There were no metaphysical testimonies to be made in clarification of this episode. I was traveling a straight line to the end of an idea. It seemed simple arithmetic. For years I'd been heading this way, moment by moment, along a perfectly true line. We reached Essex Street and walked south past the basement companies that manufactured skullcaps. We entered a tenement and started to climb stairs. There were no lights in the hallway. I smelled babies and lush garbage. The tile steps were worn at the edges. Bohack climbed behind me, about three steps back, breathing evenly into the dimness. Great Jones Street, Bond Street, Chrystie Street, Essex Street. It was sixteenth-century London we'd been slouching through in our hands-in-pockets way. I reached the final landing. Puke. Vomit. Splat. Bohack slipped past me and unlocked one of the four metal doors on the top floor, using three keys in the process.

Inside he led me along a narrow hall to a large kitchen. A man and two young girls were painting the walls a gun-metal color, using pans and rollers. Bohack gave me a glass of water and told one of the girls to clean up the mess on the landing. I followed him through another room where two men with sledgehammers were knocking down a wall. They stood in sunny ruins, clothes and bodies chalked with plaster. The third and last room looked east. It was a small room, filled with plants, feverish in the heat of three floodlights. The lone window had no curtains or blinds. Steam came clouding out of an adjacent bathroom where hot water ran in the shower. Bohack placed me in an unpainted blocklike chair and then left the room.

Plants covered the floor around the perimeter of the room and were crowded together on shelves and grew in white plastic pots hung from the ceiling and in clay pots attached to the walls with metal clips. I noted many kinds, those huge and hooded and furled on long sticks, enclosing the springs of their own alertness, or drowsy and pouched, nocturnal orchids, vines and ivies, showering ferns, palms in their rectitude, or those murky and velvet, or redolent of the limpness of old summers, or pale as lizards. A small man entered the room. He said his name was Chess. He wore flannel trousers, glazed with age, and a matching vest over a striped shirt and tie. Vest lacked a button and the tie was not centered.

"Plants are scary things," he said.

He carried an old briefcase. His hair was blondish, combed sideways almost ear to ear. He closed the door behind him, wincing at the sound of the sledgehammers.

"It's like a prison here," he said. "I don't know why they stay. People leave and then come back. Some leave twice and come back twice. You watch, I say to myself. So-and-so will leave for good next time. But they're all right here. Just like I'm right here. I'm in this room same as you. I'll tell you something about Bohack. He's not smart and he's not stupid. He doesn't have any special magnetism. His ideas just miss being interesting ideas. For a long time I couldn't figure out what made him so indispensable. Why him? What's so special? I finally figured it out. It's because he's so big. He's the biggest one. People respond to his bigness."

"Where is he?" I said.

"He's making the four o'clock check. He checks the whole floor three times a day. Tells people what to do and how to do it. Somebody has to give orders and he's the biggest. Let me ask you something. That bridge out there. Is that the Brooklyn or the Williamsburg? I've never been able to muster enough courage to ask anyone. But I feel comfortable somehow with you. There's a chemistry with you. Let me rub away some of this steam on the window and you can get a better look."

"It's the Manhattan."

"Scary," he said. "I didn't know there was a bridge called the Manhattan Bridge. All this time not knowing. Oh that's so scary. What do you think of my plants? People are usually surprised by the plants. People forget we started out as an earth-family in a completely rural and rustic environment. Interdependence of man, plant and animal. That idea still has beauty for me. So what do you think of my plants? It's dry out today so I've got the hot shower going to get some humidity in here. Plants need that. Usually I just turn on the humidifier but Spot keeps peeing in it so I've had to put it away until Bohack gets him re-toilet-trained. That's the power of names. People act in response to their names. There's a tiny sector of the human brain where the naming mechanism is located. Spot pees in my humidifier and Rex plays with a little rubber Santa Claus that goes squeak-squeak a mile a minute. Dog behavior and dog play. But don't worry, this room is sacrosanct. We don't have to be concerned about anybody coming in here who isn't authorized to do so. The orchid is a cuntlike plant. Don't you think? Menacing in its beauty. Some plants just stand there. The orchid lures a person. It draws a person inward. This room is a good room for meditation and inward thinking. It's the most inward room we have. That's as good a reason as any as to why you're here."

The door opened and Longboy stood there, left hand in his back pocket, all his weight on one leg, the left, his body slack against the door frame. Chess raised his eyebrows and Longboy responded with a series of gestures too complex to unravel. Then he backed out of the room, pulling the door closed. Chess took some clippings out of his briefcase. The window was fogged to the point of total opaqueness. I felt a sickly light sweat all over my body.

"Where's Bohack?" I said. "Is the package with him? I know you've got the damn thing."

"Pepper told us you were going on tour. Hanes told us where the record plant is."

"Hanes also turned over the product. You wouldn't have guaranteed his safety without that."

"Hanes turned over the product and Pepper agreed to test it for a straight fee. He'll probably never get paid but I doubt if he cares. He was overjoyed at this late date merely to find out what's been in that package these many weeks that's reduced us all to such deviant behavior. That begonia needs cutting back. Funny I hadn't noticed earlier."

I picked up the plant he'd indicated and threw it against the wall, using a windmill motion. Chess looked briefly at the cracked clay, leaves still embedded in lumps of earth. Then he leaned over in his chair and spread the newspaper clippings on the floor between his feet.

"Everybody's searching, you know. Everybody's trying to make the journey. But they're going about it wrong. They're seeking the wrong kind of privacy, the old privacy, never again to be found. Now here's an item about a seventy-year-old man who's sailing from Cape Hatteras to England in a skiff that's only nine feet long. It says he plans to practice yoga at sea. This one is about a Bloomington housewife who's flying from Minnesota to Australia in a balloon. Evidently she has relatives in Australia. That's the ostensible reason for the journey. We both know the real reason. A group of Methodists from Pittsburgh are setting out next month for the Sinai Desert where they intend to pray and fast for forty days and nights. It says they're being urged by their bishop to take along some kind of rations besides water but it says the group thus far has resisted the idea. Woman, sixty-two, circles world in single-engine plane. Now here's a Norwegian man who sat for two hundred and two hours in a window box on his terrace, breaking the world record by thirty-some-odd hours. We both know he wasn't interested in records. A man in Missouri spent a hundred and sixty-one days in a deep cavern. Missouri abounds in caverns. He ate canned food, he drank water, he burned over nine hundred candles. He said it's the first time in his life he wasn't bored. Sensory overload. People are withdrawing from sensory overload. Technology. Whenever there's too much technology, people return to primitive feats. But we both know that true privacy is an inner state. A limited environment is important. Yes, yes. But you can't fly off in a balloon and expect to find the answer.

The will has to urge itself to this task. The mind has to level itself across a plane of solitude. We're painting this whole floor of the building a dark gray. Not the plant room. No, no. The plant room stays white. Everything else gets painted gray."

"I just had a thought."

"The concept of a captive lunatic fringe within an organization is mine alone, my concept alone, despite what you may have heard to the contrary. Irrationality can be managed to great effect. There's power and intimidation behind every event the dog-boys are made to stage."

"Are you Dr. Pepper?" I said. "You're not, are you?"

"I'm Chess and these are my plants. Pepper is at least four inches taller than I am. You know that. Voice aside. Color of eyes aside. The man is four inches taller than I am. Pepper's feats in the realm of disguise are well known and well documented but the man can't hide four inches of muscle, bone and tissue. I'm Fred Chess, ordinary American. I used to be a theatrical producer. I went into photo offset work after that. Nothing seemed to be panning out. Look, if I were Pepper, it would mean I knew all along what kind of drug was in the package. Any long-standing intimate connection between Pepper and Happy Valley would mean that I, as Pepper, had knowledge of the drug from the very beginning. You'd have to revise everything that's happened. It would mean that I managed not only Bohack but also Hanes and Watney. If I'm Pepper, it means everything's been a lie up to now. I managed the whole thing, it means. I guided the product from hand to hand. It was my circle, point by point, the product originating at Happy Valley and ending there. It would mean that you've been the victim of the paranoid man's ultimate fear. Everything that takes place is taking place solely to mislead you. Your reality is managed by others. Logic is inside out. Events are delusions. If I were Pepper, it would mean I knew the nature of the product, I had it delivered to you, I planned and followed its course, I fabricated a Toronto meeting between Hanes and Watney, I assigned the informer to Azarian, I planted Hanes in the subway, I had Watney leave the bubble gum cards, I had Bohack bring you over here — the straight line intersecting the circle. It would mean I managed Opel."

"But there's the difference in height," I said.

"Of course there is," he said. "There's no feasible way a man can subtract four inches, is there? Not to mention eye color, voice, skin pigmentation, size of genitals and so forth. I'm Fred Chess is who I am. Fact is I have no particular respect for Dr. Pepper. The man's always been a cunt-hair away from outright quackery."

He went into the bathroom and turned off the shower, saying *ow* twice, apparently because the tap was hot. Then he opened the door and stepped into the hall. Soon the pounding stopped. Chess came back inside, followed by Bohack, Longboy and three others, men at the beck of the strongest hand, two wearing lumber jackets like mine. Beyond these six, others were gathering in the hall, male and female, standing at rest, pardonably devoid of any sign of gloom. At the edge of every disaster, people collect in affable groups to whisper away the newsless moments and wait for a messenger from the front. A small wet belch, like a child's, rippled from my lips. The window began to clear, gradually, in long vertical patches.

"It's a mind drug," Chess said. "Mind drugs affect different people different ways. They're notorious for that. Highly unpredictable. Dr. Pepper thought this stuff was atropine at first. Atropine diminishes the killer impulse. No market for that. No street market anyway. But by the time he was finished he knew it was something else. It's a drug that affects one or more areas of the left sector of the brain. Language sector. Still no market for this product. Street or otherwise. It damages the cells in one or more areas of the left sector of the human brain. Loss of speech in other words."

"I know all this. This is boring."

"Pepper was nice enough to dissolve the chemical powder with a sterile something-or-other and prepare an ampule for us. But you know what's hard to figure? Why U.S. Guv was fooling around with this stuff in the first place. Maybe they have a language warfare do partment. Maybe they think the best way to silence troublemakers is literally. That would be funny as hell if that were true. Glub, glub, glub. Or maybe Pepper was right the first time. Atropine. A tranquilizer for the killing site. But I doubt it. The man knows his dope. I give him that. Dope's his home away from home. I'm sure he was right with his second analysis."

"He'd fucking well better be right."

"Note this," Chess said. "You'll be perfectly healthy. You won't be able to make words, that's all. They just won't come into your mind the way they normally do and the way we all take for granted they will. Sounds yes. Sounds galore. But no words. No songs. You watch, I said to myself. We'll get him here and then he'll refuse to cooperate. But so far you've cooperated beautifully. It took us a great deal of time and trouble to get the drug back into our possession. Therefore we're compelled to use it. We have the drug so we're forced to administer it. Anything to say? Last words? Oh yes, we hope you'll continue to stay on Great Jones Street. We like having you nearby, yes, absolutely. Any last words?"

"Pee-pee-maw-maw," I said.

Chess eked out laughter — a petty tremble of his lips that slowly grew into a radical whining body-sound, all parts surrendering themselves to glee. Soon we were all laughing, every one of us, those in the plant room and those in the hallway, all but Bohack who stood quietly amid the vegetation, one plant touching his shoulder at the crest of its ascent. His eyes were focused and perfectly clear but it was hard to tell what he was looking at. His presence was such that only stillness could fully accommodate the cavernous power his body engendered. The room seemed to contract about him, our laughter soaking dolefully into his skin, all becoming quiet now. A phone rang in one of the other rooms. Cincinnati, I thought. All gone my mountain songs. Something in Bohack shivered invisibly at the sound of the phone and I began to realize his captivity was stricter even than mine. The news of tapes in flames brought him no joy. As the phone was answered he chose in fact not even to remain for the final stifling, in motion suddenly toward the door, crashing past two men, the lumber jacket wearers, one of them doing a little roundelay at the end of Bohack's lunge. All watched in unconnected manner this destruction of the placid air around us. He began wading through people in the hallway and soon was gone, metal door closing hard behind him as (in my mind) he stepped daintily over the vomit stain in the outer hall. Quiet returned then, a hurried calm accumulating in a kind of regional pattern, far hallway first, moving inward toward the center of the plant room. They were young, all those people gathered beyond the doorway, but haggard and slow to move, handymen, woodworkers, seamstresses, possessed of a rueful nostalgia, perhaps for the prairie womb common to them all, that land too bleak for song to live. Chess examined Longboy's fingernails for dirt and then counseled him on the proper angle of insertion, according to Dr. Pepper, forty-five to sixty degrees. Manhattan, soberest of bridges, was restored to the window in dwindling mist, never less plain, arm and broadsword of the sky. Longboy opened his medic's kit and lifted a hypodermic syringe to the pale light.

26

POLICE DOGS roamed the U-Haul trailer lots. In dock areas I found the packing houses, seeking to investigate perspectives pure as theorems, the self-mastery of these concrete structures, invulnerable to melancholy. The weather turned again, spring backing off for glassy distances of sleet, a cancellation of the body's feast of seasons, hard to wake to darkness. I dressed in old sweaters, three or four, each sufficiently torn to offer views of the one beneath but not so torn that all were visible in one wearing. I took great care to vary the layers day to day. One sweater was Opel's, a ski extravaganza, desperately out of place among the rock 'n' roll caftans at the back of the closet. I never ventured north of Cooper Square. Two deaf men had an argument near a construction shack, using their hands to curse each other, finally picking up boards and taking turns attacking. Never ventured north of Cooper Square but stood above the rivers east and west, *wod-or*, this double sound all I could fashion from the sight of sluggish currents in transit to the sea.

This one day of late rain I saw a toothless man circle a cart banked with glowing produce. He bellowed into the wind, one of nature's raw warriors, flapping around in unbuckled galoshes. A few people huddled nearby. One would now and then extend a hand toward the cart, finger-pricing, as the man wailed to the blank windows above him. It was a religious cry he produced, evocative of mosques and quaking sunsets.

RED YAPPLES GREEN YAPPLES GOLDEN YAP-PLES MAKE A YAPPLE PIE MAKE ALSO A YAPPLE STRUDEL YAPPLES YAPPLES YAPPLES BIG JUICY YAPPLES FROM THE HEART OF THE YAPPLE COUNTRY

I turned a corner and someone came out of an old hotel and ran in sputtering little steps to my side. It was the girl Skippy, Happy Valley's emissary, original bearer of the plain brown package. I kept walking and she remained alongside. We headed south and east into narrower streets, the city's older precincts, less here of surfaces, of broad lines, the women pinned in little windows, forty years flowing through an isolated second, their true lives taking place in a European pastureland. A neon digit, sizzling a bit, hung lopsided from the front of a luncheonette. It grew colder as the wind gripped in and the island tapered toward the bay. Secure I felt beneath my sweaters. Skippy coughing.

The oldest immigrants lived in tower blocks, a long way from fertile pavement, these streets now ruled by darker races of the plains. It was early afternoon and soon to rain, nondeliverance in the air, a chemical smell from the river. The bridges were cruelly beautiful in this weather, gray ladies nearly dead to all the poetry written in their names. Tall black kids in sneakers charged up out of the subway, cutting left and right across a street, fast-breaking, three on two, one of them turning now in the air, ancient stick-fingers tapping a parking sign. A man demanded money, sitting on the arm of an abandoned chair, its springs exposed. I kept forgetting Skippy was with me, then would turn to see her, body bent forward in a coughing spasm, head pointed, moving like a dog in water. We walked behind two resplendent little women wearing plastic liners over their hats, coats and shoes, one of them loudly cataloguing various items along the sidewalk.

NEWSPAPER VOMIT SHIT GLASS CARDBOARD BOTTLE SHIT SPIT NEWSPAPER GLASS SHIT GARBAGE BOTTLE CARTON BOTTLE PAPER STOCKING SHIT GARBAGE SHIT GARBAGE GARBAGE SHIT

In barbershops Latin men stood talking in buttondown shirts with collars open and sleeves folded two cuff-lengths to the lower forearm, apparel of an earlier Madison Avenue, that somber street now freshly regimented, paunchy and gay in Kool-Aid fiesta colors and Spanish sideburns. We headed west from the bridge districts and reached Chinatown, where Skippy seemed confused, apparently thinking this was San Francisco, and had to calm herself by standing for a while before the window of a fish market, watching a man guide a jagged blade up the belly of a trout as bits of fishy insides dripped onto the flaked ice. We hurried into the Criminal Court Building for warmth and sweets. The lobby was crowded and noisy, a chorus of the accused, the counter-accused, the victimized, and the lawyers, families and friends of all of these. With it all, more irate than the rest, came that special whine of minor violators. Everybody was smoking, shouting, biting down on stony Chiclets, sucking cough drops, everybody but the pimps, regal and absolute, who merely scanned the landscape, property-hunting. Behind his counter the blind newsdealer loomed as justice does, something of a self-parody, appearing to sense every nuance in the hall. He lived through his fingers, working their heat into every coin, tapping out change for the doomed and for the brothers-in-law of the doomed. We bought some candy and stood in a corner. Short purposeful men crossed the lobby on their way to and from duty, each slightly overweight and carrying the *Daily News* folded under one arm, civil servants, custodians of some kind, herders of jury members from room to room. I licked chocolate from the heel of my hand. A family of blacks surrounded a pustular lawyer, crowding his panicked grin.

Outside we saw a man with hands to eyes in the shape of binoculars and he was slowly turning on a street corner, clouds, taxis, birds, detectives, all nautically viewed by this revolving man, once drunk perhaps but well beyond that now, persevering, in full command, sensing he had found a way of dealing with the world. We walked down to the Battery, past all the forty-story objects. Wind seemed to drop directly down the flanks of buildings before ripping along the narrow streets and we passed men clutching their black hats and moving shoulder first in quick bursts of locomotion and sometimes even backward, ten or twelve men at a time, their briefcases filled with mergers, all walking backward into the wind. A rag man at the edge of the park retched into his scarf, working himself up to a moment of vast rhetoric. His seemed the type of accusation aimed at those too constricted in spirit to see the earth as a place for gods to grow, a theater of furious encounters between prophets of calamity and simple pedestrians trying to make the light.

HAND FOOT ARM GOD NOSE TOE FACE GOD LEG ARM LEG GOD SEE IT SEE IT RAIN TWAIN CAIN PAIN BRAIN SLAIN STAIN GAIN VAIN SEE IT SEE IT MOUTH EYE TEETH GOD NECK CHEST GOD SEE IT IN THE DARKNESS AND THE LIGHT

Harbors reveal a city's power, its lust for money and filth, but strangely through the haze what I distinguished first was the lone mellow promise of an island, tender retreat from straight lines, an answering sea-mound. This was the mist's illusion and the harbor's pound of flesh. Skippy tugged at licorice with her teeth, the black strands expanding between hand and jaw. She had a shaded face and she was ageless, a wanderer in cities, one of those children found after every war, picking in the rubble for scraps of food the gaunt dogs have missed. Such minds are unreclaimable but at the same time hardly dangerous and governments acknowledge this fact by providing millions of acres of postwar rubble. On our way to find a bus stop we saw the subway crowds drop into openings in the earth, on their way up the length of Manhattan or under rivers to the bourns and orchards, there to be educated in false innocence, in the rites of isolation. Perhaps the only ore of truth their lives possessed was buried in this central rock. Beyond its limits was their one escape, a dreamless sleep, no need to fear the dare to be exceptional. Dozens of pigeons swarmed around a woman tossing bread crumbs. She was in a wheelchair held at rest by a young boy, both on fire with birds, the pigeons skidding on the air, tracing the upward curve of the old woman's arm. I watched her eyes climb with the birds, all her losses made a blessing in a hand's worth of bread.

Pigeons and meningitis. Chocolate and mouse droppings. Licorice and roach hairs. Vermin on the bus we took uptown. I wondered how long I'd choose to dwell in these middle ages of plague and usury, living among traceless men and women, those whose only peace was in shouting ever more loudly. Nothing tempted them more than voicelessness. But they shouted. Transient population of thunderers and hags. They dragged through wet streets speaking in languages older than the stones of cities buried in sand. Beds and bedbugs. Men and lice. Gonococcus curling in the lap of love.

We rode past an urban redevelopment project. Machine-tooth shovels clawed past half-finished buildings stuck in mud, tiny balconies stapled on. All spawned by realtor-kings who live in the sewers. Skippy coughed blood onto the back of her hand. The bus panted over cobblestones and I studied words drawn in fading paint on the sides of buildings. Brake and front end service. Wheel alignment. Chain and belt. Pulleys, motors, gears. Sheet-metal machinery. Leather remnants. Die cutting and precision measuring. Cuttings and job lots. Business machines. Threads, woolens, laces. Libros en español. We left by the back door and Skippy went back to whatever she was doing (or dealing) in that hotel. Rain blew across the old streets. The toothless man was still at his cart, a visitation from sunken regions, not caring who listened or passed, his cries no less cadenced than the natural rain.

YOU'RE BUYING I'M SELLING YAPPLES YAPPLES YAPPLES

The bed remains at the center of the room. Visitors are rare now and I begin to feel I'm sinking into history. After Essex Street I spent weeks of deep peace. I lived in true eunuchry, bed-watching, forced to respond to nothing. Having no words for the things around me affected even my movements across the room. I walked more slowly, as though in fear of objects, all things with names unknown to me. Some of the careless passion people feel for unteachable children began to communicate itself from one part of my mind to another. I was unreasonably happy, subsisting in blessed circumstance, thinking of myself as a kind of living chant. I made interesting and original sounds. I looked out the window and moaned (quietly) at the lumbering trucks below and at the painters and sculptors now occupying windows across the way, placid faces suspended over Great Jones Street. But whatever else it was, the drug was less than lasting in its effect. *Mouth* was the first word to reach me, dropping from one speech mechanism to the other. It happened while I was looking at my face in the mirror, examining its strange parts, *hanu, ous, leb, oog, nakka,* and when I opened my mouth out came the word for that part, word instead of sound, *mouth,* startling me. More words followed and when I spoke them aloud the sound waves reached my brain in proper coded notes and I was able to comprehend what had passed between my tongue and inner ear. Soon all was normal, a return to prior modes. This was my double defeat, first a chance not taken to reappear in the midst of people and forces made to my design and then a second enterprise denied, alternate to the first, permanent withdrawal to that unimprinted level where all sound is silken and nothing erodes in the mad weather of language. Several weeks of immense serenity. Then ended. But I see no reason to announce the news. Let viscid history suck me down a bit. When the season is right I'll return to whatever is out there. It's just a question of what sound to make or fake. Meanwhile the rumors accumulate. Kidnap, exile, torture, self-mutilation and death. The most beguiling of the rumors has me living among beggars and syphilitics, performing good works, patron saint of all those men who hear the river-whistles sing the mysteries and who return to sleep in wine by the south wheel of the city.

FOR THE BEST IN PAPERBACKS, LOOK FOR THE

In every corner of the world, on every subject under the sun, Penguin represents quality and variety—the very best in publishing today.

For complete information about books available from Penguin—including Puffins, Penguin Classics, and Arkana—and how to order them, write to us at the appropriate address below. Please note that for copyright reasons the selection of books varies from country to country.

In the United Kingdom: Please write to *Dept. JC, Penguin Books Ltd, FREEPOST, West Drayton, Middlesex UB7 0BR.*

If you have any difficulty in obtaining a title, please send your order with the correct money, plus ten percent for postage and packaging, to *P.O. Box No. 11, West Drayton, Middlesex UB7 0BR*

In the United States: Please write to *Consumer Sales, Penguin USA, P.O. Box 999, Dept. 17109, Bergenfield, New Jersey 07621-0120.* VISA and MasterCard holders call 1-800-253-6476 to order all Penguin titles

In Canada: Please write to *Penguin Books Canada Ltd, 10 Alcorn Avenue, Suite 300, Toronto, Ontario M4V 3B2*

In Australia: Please write to *Penguin Books Australia Ltd, P.O. Box 257, Ringwood, Victoria 3134*

In New Zealand: Please write to *Penguin Books (NZ) Ltd, Private Bag 102902, North Shore Mail Centre, Auckland 10*

In India: Please write to *Penguin Books India Pvt Ltd, 706 Eros Apartments, 56 Nehru Place, New Delhi 110 019*

In the Netherlands: Please write to *Penguin Books Netherlands bv, Postbus 3507, NL-1001 AH Amsterdam*

In Germany: Please write to *Penguin Books Deutschland GmbH, Metzlerstrasse 26, 60594 Frankfurt am Main*

In Spain: Please write to *Penguin Books S. A., Bravo Murillo 19, 1° B, 28015 Madrid*

In Italy: Please write to *Penguin Italia s.r.l., Via Felice Casati 20, I-20124 Milano*

In France: Please write to *Penguin France S. A., 17 rue Lejeune, F-31000 Toulouse*

In Japan: Please write to *Penguin Books Japan, Ishikiribashi Building, 2-5-4, Suido, Bunkyo-ku, Tokyo 112*

In Greece: Please write to *Penguin Hellas Ltd, Dimocritou 3, GR-106 71 Athens*

In South Africa: Please write to *Longman Penguin Southern Africa (Pty) Ltd, Private Bag X08, Bertsham 2013*